This Book Belongs To:

Goliath Catfish

Scott T. Gill

Miss you in Gili
English.

Published by Glass Page Books

P.O. Box 333, Signal Mountain, Tennessee 37377
http://www.glasspagebooks.com

First Edition
Cover Design by P.L. Alexander
Illustration by Jordan Alexander

Library of Congress Control Number: 2012943770

Gill, Scott T.
Goliath Catfish

Summary: Albert McClune is bigger than most kids in his neighborhood. He dreams of
being his family's hero, to turn their fortunes, and return the happiness lost with his brother
Pete. But Albert is crippled by fear and shame. Fleeing home, he meets Elijah Amos Fortune
Jones, an odd boy who takes him on a treasure hunt deep into the city sewers and uncharted
caves. They face a voodoo priest, swim in rat-infested tunnels, and engage in a deadly race for
the lost ransom of Machine Gun Kelly. Albert is forced to be courageous or lose everything he
loves as he faces the guilt that has cut him down to size. ...but beware the man-sized catfish!

ISBN: 978-0-9852558-2-4

Young Adult Fiction, Action/Adventure, Suspense

Printed in the United States of America

Independent
Press

Tennessee, U.S.A

Dedicated to:

Philip, Aidan, and Brennen. You guys inspired so much of these characters.

To my sweet little Ireland, my early morning companion through most of the writing.

And finally, to my wife and best friend, Angie. If it were not for your encouragement, I would have never started writing.

Chapter One

Kudzu was a nuisance, winding and tangling all over the forest, tripping the feet, rustling, pulling. It made hunting especially hard, except that it could camouflage, which is exactly what Albert was counting on as he stalked the rabbit. He was going through a lot of trouble to kill it, but it was necessary.

Albert inched along, threading his husky body through the vines, sweat pouring down his forehead as he edged his left arm, right arm, then his legs slowly through the green blanket. The brown jackrabbit settled before a huge oak. The old tree clung by its roots to an eroding bluff, hanging there like a man grasping the edge of a cliff. Stopping beneath its hairy roots, the rabbit then turned and bound along the out-cropping of the bluff and froze still—the perfect shot. Birds squelched their singing; the woods became silent.

Sliding the rifle up along his side, weaving through the tangles and leaves, he rested the scarred wooden stock against his bare shoulder. His grandfather had smuggled it from the Great War to America during the Irish exodus. It was a means to fill their stomachs, and it was the family's one and only treasure.

Funny how something as small as a rabbit could be so important. Bringing it home would elevate Albert, making him a hero like Pete. Albert thought about a time when, amidst his father's praises, Pete had towered in the doorway, lifting stringers full of dripping catfish.

Albert hated catfish but not because of taste.

He aimed the gun, his left eye squeezed tightly, and he peered down the long barrel that jutted just inches from his forearm.

"Move a little more, come on, just a little," he whispered and licked along the edges of his mouth; his stomach growled like a moaning beggar. The last two days consisted of cabbage soup—if it could be called that since it was closer to cabbage-cooked-to-death-in-salty-water soup. Albert wanted more than that, wanted meat.

He felt the trigger, applied the pressure, and heard a scream.

The rabbit paused then leaped.

CRACK!

Bark shattered from the tree, and the rabbit disappeared in a shake of kudzu.

Missed!

Jumping up, Albert worked the bolt and scanned the forest floor.

"Hey! Who you shooting at?" echoed a voice.

In the bottoms, just beyond the grasping tree, pointed a familiar figure.

"You're a dead man!" he shouted, darting up the bluff.

It was time to run. Albert could not get caught. His ragged overalls were so ripped on the cuffs that the strings tangled on the overgrowth. He pounded each foot up and down to work out of the knee-high kudzu. He had to get out into the open before he was overrun by his pursuer. Jumping, he lifted each foot higher than the other.

Hurry, faster, go... go... go!

The pursuer's Comanche whoops grew louder. Although the end of the kudzu field was in sight, it would not relent with the tussling and grabbing at his legs—a leafy green octopus in league with a crazed stalker. Albert glanced back. He knew the attacker's identity: Buddy Clines.

Buddy was erratic, dangerous. Caught alone in the woods with him was like being near a rabid wolf. He had once beaten a black kid, poured molasses and feathers all over him, and hung him by the back of the pants on a tree limb. Hours later the kid was found.

Suddenly silence permeated, no more sounds of running or war whoops, just a creepy emptiness that often haunted a forest. Albert turned and scanned the bosky bluffs. Nothing. But he could not breathe easy. Buddy rarely relented.

Albert jogged on and reached a trail that twisted in and out of pines and thick oaks. Then he scurried up a steep incline and edged a bluff that had been cut during a flood; the drop neared fifteen feet and a creek wound through the gravelly bottom. Side stepping some roots, he crossed around an old hickory tree and felt a shove on his shoulder, knocking him off balance. Dirt gave way and dropped from under his feet, and he careened over the eroded edge. Buddy smiled down at Albert, but Albert's stomach felt like it was rushing up to his throat, his body falling, falling...

THUD!

Air exploded from his lungs and pain shocked across his back from the stabbing of broken branches, the scraping of rocks, and the burning of his raw shirtless skin. Careening into a prickly bush, the rifle slammed and fired. Its crack echoed over the bluffs and through the Mississippi River valley. Albert lie gasping, willing himself to breathe. The warm ditch water wet his overalls.

"Wooohooo! That was quite a fall, yessir!" Buddy cackled. The ruffian swaggered down the snaking trail along the bluff. He grabbed some hairy tree roots along the weathered edge to steady his gait. Strutting up to Albert, he kneeled and smiled. His stained teeth hung crooked with the front ones missing, leaving a gaping black hole. His eyes were ice blue and sweat beaded on his forehead.

"Got to watch that last step," Buddy spat. "It's a doozy."

The sweet, acrid odor of tobacco filled Albert's nose, and brown saliva dribbled down Buddy's freckled chin. His blond, close-shaven head bore little scars from past scuffles. He peered at Albert then reached down and grabbed the bib of his overalls, lifting Albert's big torso off the ground.

"You shot at me, maggot!"

He punched Albert in the face. The agony was immediate. It burned. Water filled his eyes as the pain poured around his cheeks. Warm blood trickled from his nose, winding down to his mouth. He tasted its salt.

"I shot at a rab—"

Buddy punched him again. This one was worse, numbing the teeth. Albert spat blood.

"DON'T TALK TO ME, JACKASS," Buddy shouted, shoving Albert back to the ground.

Still wheezing from the pummeling, Albert started to cry.

"Wait a cotton-pickin' minute. I seen you before. Your daddy works at the docks for mine. Yeah, I seen you walkin' with him," Buddy said, scratching his head as his face lit up. "Hey, you're the one with that nut-case brother." Laughing, Buddy shook his head. "Does he still slobber and talk to himself? I heard that when the men drug him to Bolivar, he foamed at the mouth and messed his drawers."

Buddy turned and ambled his way to the thorny brush where the rifle had landed.

Albert's neck and face burned, and he wanted to be back in the kudzu where he could hide from the world. Better yet: he wished the bullet had actually hit the unintended target.

Buddy turned his face to Albert and grinned as he sunk his arm inside the brush. Then he pulled himself loose, sliding the gun out from between the thorny branches. Albert's heart beat faster.

"Lookie what I found. Some stupid hunter dropped his gun!"

Albert rolled off his back. "That's mine..."

Buddy spun, aimed the rifle, and worked the bolt. "I'll shoot your ass as I'm standin' here, big boy. Finders keepers is the rule 'round here."

"But it's..." Albert stared down the barrel and bowed his head. "Please... it's all we got."

Tears rolled down his cheek. The hunting rifle was the last precious thing they owned.

"I've never seen a leprechaun kid as big as you. Why don't you and your Pope-lovin' family go back to the potato farm you came from?"

Buddy lowered the gun a little and turned it on its side, checking it out.

"This must've been in the war—killed some Germans I bet. My daddy says Adolf ain't so bad a guy as everybody thinks." He fingered the stock, smiling like a kid at Christmas. "If Adolf was here, he'd take care of you micks and the coons, that's for damn sure."

Albert wobbled to his feet as Buddy ogled the rifle. He stepped closer, pleading, "Please..."

Buddy whipped around and slammed the butt into his gut. Albert gasped again, losing the air his lungs had finally begun to enjoy. His legs buckled and he collapsed.

"You're pitiful! I should just give you the bullet, save the world some air."

Albert wheezed.

"And don't you even think about tellin' your daddy about this. I'm sure he'd like to keep loading barges for mine, if you know what I mean." Buddy sniffed and forged some tears, "Daddy, I...I was shot at today by one of those filthy micks." Then he grinned at his piece of theater.

He turned and took a step but turned back and aimed the rifle. Albert knelt in the dirt and rocks. Was this going to be it: a bullet in the head to accompany a bludgeon to the gut?

"Oh, and don't let me catch you in these woods again, or I'll be the one shootin'," Buddy said, and pulling an imaginary trigger, he made a firing sound and simulated the kick. Then he spun and scrambled up the bluff, stood at attention, and saluted. As he disappeared into the trees, his hollering and celebrating echoed in the bottoms.

Albert sobbed and yanked a clump of grass, throwing it. He had lost the last thing his family treasured and his only chance of being the family hero. Buddy had stolen everything.

Albert picked himself up and wiped the dirt off of his bare shoulders. Dust and rocks ran down his legs, and his face and clothes were caked with blood-mixed mud. If he returned home, his dad would know he had been beaten up—it was not the first time.

"With your size, m' boy, you should be doin' the beatin'," he would say in his fading Irish accent. "Softer than a sheep," he would mumble as he turned.

Soft, just like a big old sheep.

It would only be a matter of time before Dad noticed the rifle gone and only a little more before he learned the truth. Then bad would turn to worse. Sean McClune was a true Irishman: fond of drink and hot of temper. He would enter into a rant and empty a bottle. Then he would need a fight, and Butch Clines would be the first contender. A fight and then a firing, that was the future. From there they would call the streets home and salty cabbage water a delicacy.

He could not go home, not now. Going home would bring a curse on a family whose luck had run out. For everyone's good, he had to run, and for Albert, running was the easiest way to solve problems. He was a burden anyway, and with all that had happened to Pete, leaving would lighten everybody's load. He was, after all, a soft sheep—a soft sheep without wool.

He approached a clearing. Across an overgrown field, a dirt road snaked in the distance, and a cluster of shotgun houses nestled in a flood plain beyond the tall river bluff. The dockworkers dwelled there, just a short walk from the cobblestone ports and the mighty Mississippi that served up the grain-filled barges. "Muddy" was the best way to describe the river's appearance, and on its banks, Memphis loomed—the Blues City—full of music and mayhem.

Albert had only been in the city a few times, but he believed it was his only hope. He could not hide in the woods because Buddy had the gun. He had no choice. He had to escape, and at least in the city there was opportunity to fill his growling stomach. He could beg maybe or even steal in the worst case, but home was not an option.

Wiping his eyes, he trudged through the waist high grass that swayed and caressed as the hot wind blew. He loped down a long hill toward the river. There was no hurry because he had no hope, or at least that is what he thought. There would be one stop along the way: a place he always went to when he needed to think. And that was one thing he must do if he was not going home.

Chapter Two

Broken bottles and split tin cans littered the rocky bank that Albert sidestepped. Finally, he reached his spot—a little ledge that ran beside the mouth of a sewer pipe.

Nobody visited the place. It was a rocky ravine where three sewer pipes converged and emptied, shuttling rainwater from the Memphis streets into a stony ditch. The ditch wound around some woods and emptied into the Wolf River, a feeder of the Mississippi. On a stormy day, the water gushed from the pipes and flooded the ravine—swirling and bubbling—and the refuse dipped and jumped over the waves like little rafts. However, on a hot day, the water trickled from the pipes with melted paper and algae hanging from the pig-iron grates that guarded the openings.

Albert found some round, smooth rocks and skipped them in the stagnating puddles. Why did he not just level down on Buddy? Why did he run?

He always ran, ever since Pete. He chucked a huge rock that splashed in a stinking mosquito pool. Tears filled his eyes and ran down his cheeks.

"COWARD," he said and flung another rock.

"Why you sad?" a raspy voice asked behind him.

Albert jumped and wiped his face with his dirty arm. On top of one of the pipes stood a bony black kid. Matted hair capped his little round head. His high forehead shaded big eyes and a pug nose. He had a large mouth with big white teeth—the front two bucked.

Whites did not associate with blacks, and even Albert's family, regardless of being poor and "dirty" Irish, kept to themselves. Most of the blacks nearby lived in the Shanties—a cluster of tin-roofed lean-tos by the river. A potholed gravel road, scattered with gin bottles and skeletal dogs, led the way to the shacks.

"Why you sad?" he repeated.

"Just get out of here," Albert snapped. "Leave me alone."

"This here is the property of the city of Memphis, and I'm a bona fide citizen. I can be here jus' like you, and I ain't going nowhere." The kid crossed his arms and spat on the pipe where he was standing.

Albert wheeled around and sat down, covering his face with his hands.

"What's yo name?" the kid asked.

"Albert."

"Ooooooh. That's a royal name, an old name, a name for princes, kings, and potentates."

"It's cursed," Albert replied.

"Maybe. Prince Albert died of that coughin' sickness, but other than that, he was a pretty lucky fella."

"What are you talking about?"

"Prince Albert...married a queen...good man I hear. Ain't you in school?"

"Sometimes."

"Wish I could go," he yammered, spitting constantly.

"What's your name?" Albert asked, finding the boy intriguing.

The boy put his hands on his hips and smiled.

"Me? I am Elijah Amos Fortune Jones. Elijah is the name of a prophet of God. Amos Fortune was a slave that bought his freedom. Jones is the name of a slaver that once owned my great grand pap." Elijah looked down at Albert and asked, "Why you think yo name is cursed?"

"Because I'm poor and everything I do makes it worse."

Elijah turned and raised his right hand as if to gesture to a crowd. Clearing his throat and spitting he said, "But I's, bein' poor, have only my dreams. I have my dreams under yo feet; tread softly, 'cause you tread on my dreams."

"You're nuts," Albert said, but he found Elijah amusing and most definitely the strangest kid he had ever encountered.

"That was W.B. Yeats. He was a poet who died a couple of years ago. Prince Albert, you may be poor, we's all poor, but we can still have dreams. What's yo's?"

"I'm not a prince, and I don't know about dreams," Albert said.

"Sure you do. Deep down inside everybody gots 'em. I'm gonna be mayor of this here town," Elijah said, jumping off the pipe and sitting next to Albert.

"That's impossible."

"Careful now, don't tread on my dream. It's mine." Elijah glared into Albert's eyes, but Albert could not face him.

Elijah leaned close and said, "Now tell ol' Elijah who tread down yo dreams?"

Almost magically, Elijah pulled the words from him: "Buddy Clines, life, dumb Irish luck."

"I don't know about no Irish luck, but I do know about that white devil Buddy Clines. What he do?"

"He took my rifle."

"How'd he take it?"

"He just took it. He beat me down and took it. It was the last thing we had that was worth anything. I hunted with it. Now I can't go home."

"Take it back."

"What?

"Take it back," Elijah repeated.

"I can't."

Elijah lowered his head and snickered.

"You're laughing at me," Albert said and stood, his face reddened, "you stupid ni—"

"Now don't be a sayin' somethin' we'd both regret, Prince Albert. Elijah ain't your enemy. I's just wondering if you've seen yourself lately?"

"What do you mean?"

"Albert, you is huge and you had the gun! Ain't nobody should be able to take nothing from you— especially Clines. He should be the one here cryin' on my shoulder." Elijah grabbed some gravel and side-armed a flat piece into the trickling stream below. The rock spun and splashed the puddle once, bouncing back into the air to come down a second time—a two-skipper. Albert calmed and stared into the distance.

"You is in good Irish luck now; I'm a lookin' for a business partner," Elijah said and slid from the ledge and walked down to the bottom of the ditch. He inspected the pig-iron grate on the sewer pipe mouth.

Hardened algae clung to it, having been filtered from a heavy flood. It had been several days with no rain, so now the water passing through was a mere trickle.

"What?"

"I need a partner of good size, and I bet you would like to help your family. It'll give you somethin' to bring home, to make up for the rifle." He pulled and tugged on the grate.

"What's your business?"

"Treasure huntin'."

Albert snickered this time.

"You think I kiddin'?"

"I think you're crazy."

"I found a map. Been studyin' it for some time. There is treasure, and I'm lookin' for a partner. Take it or leave it."

"How do you know it's a real map?"

Elijah looked around, walked up to Albert, and leaned in close to whisper, "I found it on a murdered man."

Albert's jaw dropped. "Where?"

"Let's not be yappin' a bunch out here 'bout it," Elijah said, looking around and staring at the three pipes. He seemed obsessed with the sewers. The water had gone from a trickle to a pour, splashing out around the rocks, swirling and sucking through the gulley. A salamander squirreled around in the new "river" hunting mosquitoes. "So, are you in? We partners?"

Albert was not sure. The old familiar fear boiled in his belly. It was not what he had planned when he first thought to run away from home.

"Whatcha gonna do Prince Albert? If you can't go back home, where you gonna go? You can only run so long. You have a chance here to make it right. Why not take it?"

Albert stared into the rising pools that bubbled from the sewer rush. He saw Pete in that river screaming and pulling and fighting with all his might.

"Fine, I'll go."

"All right," Elijah said. He stood and spit in his hand and offered it to Albert. "Go on, you spit in your hand, and we's swear a solemn oath to one another."

Elijah had a skinny, long hand. A bubbly wet splat gathered in his palm and formed a drop. Albert spat in his own hand and grabbed Elijah's, shaking, sealing the partnership.

"We's promises to helps one another and to not ditch each other no matter the situation, and we's will split the loot fifty-fifty. May the Lord infest our beds with bees and our armpits with fleas if we break this solemn oath. You swear?"

Albert snickered and said, "I swear."

"Now, we got to get supplies. All adventurers need stuff for their journey. You gotta flashlight?"

"An old lantern, I think, but it's at home."

"That'll work. Go and get it...and a burlap sack too."

"Elijah, I can't. I can't go back."

"Your first mistake is sayin' 'I can't.' You can and you must. If you ever want a chance at goin' home for good, you gotta. We gonna see tougher things than that soon enough, and we'll be wanting to say 'can't' then. So, we can't start out saying it now."

Albert doubted that they would see rougher things, but adventurers needed supplies, and Elijah appeared to have nothing more than the rags on his back. Nevertheless, fumbling around the shed for the lantern without getting caught would be challenging.

"The Greek heroes endured all kinda tests to prove themselves. This is your test, Prince Albert, now get to it," Elijah smiled, "and if you find something for me to eat, I sure be appreciative."

***

Albert's cracker-box house perched on a small hill, standing a little taller than the other homes along the gravel road. Hopefully, the thicket that clumped on the side was enough to hide him. He would stage his assault there, checking that no one was around before he streaked across the yard to search the shed.

Greek heroes and their tests... Miss Thatcher had taught him about them: Hercules and his favorite, Atlas. Ironically though, like Atlas, Albert felt like he held a world on his shoulders—like the fate of his family was in his hands. Maybe it was other people's expectations of him. People constantly commented on his size like it was supposed to make him special. The only thing that Albert saw about himself was "big soft sheep."

The house was a shotgun type, which meant it was three times as long as it was wide. White paint peeled off the sides, the flecks speckling the ground. The front porch was too skinny even for a couple of rocking chairs. The walls, paper thin, did little to divide the home, and at night, he overheard his mom weeping or his dad ranting over Butch Clines, lost shifts, and Pete.

Albert crawled through the thicket and prepared to dart toward the old woodshed, but his dad emerged from the backside of the house, stomping toward it. He stumbled inside the crooked doorway and the door closed. He slammed it back open, holding a broken handled hammer in his fist, his brown eyes bloodshot and his whiskers long. Disappearing on the other side of the house, he pounded away, probably patching the hole that termites had eaten. As soon as the hammer hit, Albert dashed to the shed.

An old engine collected dust in the corner. Saw horses were collapsed on their sides from the weight of scrap wood, their legs spread like a giraffe's. Albert scanned the nail-blanketed workbench, but the lantern was nowhere in the piles of bolts and nuts. He had only seconds before Dad returned.

The lantern hung on a rusty nail between empty paint cans. Albert crept over and then realized the silence; the hammering had stopped. The crunching of footsteps in gravel signaled that Dad neared the door.

Albert snagged the lantern, grabbed a box of matches, and slipped into the dark storeroom that housed Mom's canning jars. Pulling the door shut, he left a small crack to see. Dad entered and threw the hammer in a bucket that clanged when it hit. He reached in his back pocket and pulled out a flat bottle, spun the top, and took a swig. Albert smelled the sweetness of the whisky and it almost made him sick. Dad wiped his mouth and looked toward the storeroom, glaring. Albert froze.

"Who left the damn door open?" he slurred, slamming it shut.

The room was dark. Something crept along Albert's shoulders, a spider, but he could not holler or jump, so he brushed his clothes and shook off the chills.

He heard nothing else and assumed Dad had left—gone to drink some more. He cracked the door and exited the storeroom. A dirty potato sack crumpled in a corner so he grabbed it and shook off the dust. The earthy powder clouded and tickled his nose, making him want to sneeze. He had to get out of there before he gave away his presence. Holding back the sneeze was almost as impossible as blocking the mighty Mississippi, so he darted out of the shed, but caught himself and went back into the storeroom. The shelves were empty except for a few pickle jars.

"Figures."

He snatched a jar, stuffed it in the sack, and headed back to the wash and to the adventure that awaited him after his test.

Chapter Three

Like a victor trumpeting the spoils of war,
Albert lifted the lantern high as he stumbled down the
ravine to the wash. He had succeeded, but Elijah was
missing. Albert's neck burned and sweat broke on his
forehead; he grit his teeth. It was all a trick. That piece
of shanty trash was probably giggling about the big,
dumb white kid that believed a treasure hunt story.

Soft, *stupid* sheep.

Albert dropped his hands and turned to go.

"Hey! You ain't getting cold feets are you?"

Elijah stumbled out of the woods on the other
side of the gully dragging a large, knobby limb.

"Uh... um...I thought you had left—tricked me
or something."

As Elijah yanked the branch, the leaves rustled and small limbs popped. He reached the pipes and started snapping off the smaller branches. "I made an oath, Prince Albert, and once I makes an oath, I keeps it. Why you doubting?"

"I don't know... I..."

"'Cause I'm a negro?" He put his calloused foot on the big end and pulled up on the branch. It cracked as if it were in a fire.

"No. I...I'm sorry."

Elijah paused. Albert feared he had already damaged their partnership. Then Elijah smiled. "Aww, it's all right. You gots any food? My stomach done think my throat is cut."

Albert laid down the lantern and pulled a mason jar out of the burlap sack. "These are my mom's hot pickles. They're about all we have left," he said and twisted the top. Elijah jumped in the ankle deep gulley and waded across.

"You can finish off that branch while I have a snack." Elijah reached in and grabbed a long, pale pickle, vinegar and spices dripping, and lowered it into his open mouth. He smiled, chewing, then frowned, tears welling in his eyes.

"Oh, they're a little spicy," Albert said and snapped shoots off the branch, finally leaving a limbless log.

Elijah jumped back in the gully, coughing and spitting, and hit his knees as if begging for forgiveness. "Oh, Lordy! Sweet Jesus! My mouth is in the seventh ring of HELL!"

He scooped the sewer water to his red lips and spat over and over. He slapped the water and jumped on one leg then the other–his eyes squinting tight. He resembled a Cherokee warrior dancing around a campfire. Albert giggled and then dropped the branch in a full-blown laugh.

"Lord, how did you get so big eatin' dem things?"

"Never swallowed one," Albert cackled. "We spit them out when mom's not looking. Dad says they're good and messy, so they're best eaten on the porch, but it really just gives us a place to spit. She thinks we love them and keeps making them."

Still coughing, Elijah got to his feet and lifted the large branch. "We better get goin' 'fore someone comes around."

"Why the branch?"

"This is why you is the best partner. I need you to take this branch and jimmy that grate open."

"The sewer grate? Why?"

Elijah rolled his eyes. "Cause that's where the treasure lies." He lifted his hands and stared in the sky and shouted, "Lord, give this boy ears to hear and eyes to see!"

Albert lowered his head.

"That center pipe is the one we is needin'."

Albert ambled over and peered through the gridiron. It was dark, a darkness that was thick, worse than the river bottoms on a moonless night. He grabbed a bar and shook it. It rattled in its brackets, the sound echoing off into the void.

He could forget it all and just run away. Yet, he remembered what Elijah had said about the oath and the bees, and so far, Elijah had kept his word. Albert forced himself to pick up the thick branch. Poking one end through the pig-iron grate, he pushed with the other end. The rusty bars pulled away from the mouth and the branch cracked.

Elijah examined the mossy bars and said, "Just a little more, the brackets is almost broke."

Albert shoved one more time. The wood popped and splintered, and the grate swung open, but Albert kept going and stumbled into the ditch. He jumped up a bit embarrassed, his knees wet, but Elijah paid no attention. He had set the lantern inside the pipe mouth and lifted the glass.

"You remember a match?" he asked.

Albert padded his pockets for the box he had snagged and said, "We'll get soaked in there."

"Well, it don't matter much; we ain't dressed for Sunday meetin' no ways."

Albert noticed that his denim overalls looked like a king's clothes compared to the mud-stained t-shirt and ripped trousers Elijah wore.

"You think there's alligators?" Albert asked.

Elijah struck the match and lit the lantern and gave the box back to Albert. "If they is, we'll just head down another pipe. Gators is slow, I hear. Besides, that why I gots you."

He handed Albert the lantern and pushed himself up into the mouth. Grabbing the light and the burlap bag, he motioned for Albert to follow.

Albert did not know if Elijah meant for him to wrestle gators, or if he would be their food while Elijah escaped. "You're kidding, right? There ain't gators, right?"

Albert crawled into the pipe. It was pitch black except for the lantern light. It was the kind of dark so deep that if the lantern burned out, Albert would not be able to see his hand in front of his face. Cobwebs floated from above and tickled his neck. Water trickled and bubbled. The pipe was not big enough for him to stand, so he squat and shuffled like Elijah, using his hands for balance. Their splashing and sloshing echoed through the labyrinth.

At first the water felt good and cool after such a hot morning, but it was not long before the constant wetness wore on the nerves. Sewer silt was slick and slimy like wet coffee grounds that settled in a cup, and it smelled of rotten eggs when stirred. Cockroaches dribbled along the smooth concrete walls. Albert slapped his neck at the hairy feeling of one scampering down his overalls.

Elijah stopped and turned, saying, "Here's a good spot."

He set the lantern down in the shallow water. The base stuck in the mud and the water flowed around it. He unbuttoned his front pocket and produced a ragged piece of thick paper. It was a torn map as evidenced by the frayed edges, but instead of roads and lakes, this map had a grid pattern covered by a ton of checks, marks, and arrows.

"It looks like a mess. How do you figure it's a treasure map?"

"It's part of a sewer map. I think them marks are little check-offs, like the map owner was goin' places and looking for somthin'. It seems to me that whoever this map belonged to, they were searching the sewer for somthin' important."

"How do you know that it wasn't just some sewer worker's map?"

"Cause the dead fella I found it on was no worker. He looked like a hobo."

"Maybe it was an accident?"

"And Julius Ceasar jus' so happened to of walked backwards into Brutus' knife! The man's throat was cut," Elijah said and ran his finger across his neck. "His head was nearly off, hands stiff and cold, still clinching the map like he had yanked it away. You see those words along that edge?"

Albert squinted in the pale light. Inscribed on the side was "GK Barnes."

"Who is GK Barnes?" Albert asked.

"The only name I know that fits is George Kelly Barnes."

"Who's that?"

"Boy, don't you know noth'in? George Kelly Barnes was a bank robber, bootlegger, even kidnapped a fella; he was famous around these parts. They called him 'Machine Gun' Kelly. He was arrested here a few years back, 1933, I think. My pa remembers it well. Says folks yapped about it all over the city."

Elijah folded the map and tucked it away and scooted around in the water and mud, picking in the silt.

Albert did not like the sound of it all. A man was nearly beheaded, and Elijah had a kidnapper's map.

"You think he's connected with this map?" Albert asked.

"He is definitely connected."

"What makes you so sure this map leads to treasure?" Albert persisted.

"Cause anything marked up with a bank robber's name on it has somethin' to do with money... there, found some!" Elijah lifted up a muddy coin.

He had to be crazy. Sure, it was not the treasure Elijah spoke of, but it was exciting to find money right under his feet. Albert mimicked Elijah and dug around in the silt. He wished he had thought of exploring the sewers before, if for no other reason but to find a constant flow of change. Unearthing a nickel, he scooped water over it to wash it off.

"What do you think happened to the other half of the map?"

"Albert, you're sure full of questions. I ain't positive about anything, but we is gonna find out soon enough. Now, keep scoopin' around, and see if you find some more money. We gotta go see a fortune teller."

"What? Who?"

"We got to get some information. The Greeks used to ask the oracle at Delphi. We's gonna talk to Ol' Zephaniah, but he's got to have payment."

Albert dug around and found some more change, two nickels and a mass of pennies. If they never found the treasure, he was still determined he would come right back to this spot to find more coins. He put the ones he had found in the burlap sack.

"So, you know this man?"

"Shoot naw, I's only knows about him. Nobody really *knows* Zephaniah. Can't really get close to a voodoo priest. He's as mean as a polecat and jus' as dangerous. We gots to be careful."

Puttering around, he found a few more coins and placed them in Albert's sack, saying, "But he knows everything 'bout everybody in Memphis, and he may jus' give us our fortunes if we pay him enough money. Thank ya Jesus! Found me a quarter." Elijah lifted the large coin as silt ran down his arm.

Albert's stomach twisted and he had a shiver. He was now along for the ride, and although he had nothing to lose, he was scared. However, if that map was a map to hidden riches, it may save his family. He just was not so sure about meeting this Zephaniah.

He dug around faster and moved up the pipe as he continued to find junk of all sorts: shell casings from a gun, rusty nails, and a Zippo lighter. It was a small treasure.

He had always wanted a Zippo lighter, but Momma had never allowed it. He loved to watch the men in the barbershop, long cigars clinched in their teeth, flicking the top open and ripping the flint wheel that produced a bold flame. He shook it. It was full of fuel unless it had taken on water. He flicked the top off. Mud clogged the wheel. He dug it out and spun it. Small sparks flew. It was a keeper. He slipped it into his breast pocket thinking it would surely come in handy and maybe even bring a little luck. If he was about to meet a voodoo priest, he would need all he could get.

Elijah sloshed over and asked, "How much you got?"

"About fifty cents."

"Good. That'll make 'bout two dollars. It should be enough. Let's get going."

Elijah led the way, and they reached an intersection of pipes. He brought the lantern close to the map, studied it, and peered around at the different options. He stretched the lantern in the opening of the pipe that went to their right and again eyed the map.

"This is it."

They turned down the pipe. Elijah's shadowy shape was all that was visible against the glowing light. He suddenly jumped and yelled, "RAT!"

The varmint skittered right toward Albert along the pipe. Albert hated rats. He periodically spotted them in the shed, their black marble eyes and whip-like tails giving him the chills. Hopefully, they would not see a whole lot of them, but that was only wishful thinking. Sewers and rats came hand in hand.

A fortune teller was someone he had always wanted to visit. He wanted to know his future, but he did not know about this Zephaniah person. How was he mean? Danger was not what Albert sought on this adventure.

"We're here," Elijah said, pointing.

Light beamed into the pipe ahead and grew with every step and slosh. Albert's eyes had grown accustomed to the dark, and he struggled to focus at the newfound brightness. A fallen tree barred most of the opening and was cemented by a concoction of silt and leaves. The only way out was through a small opening in the top half of the pipe. Elijah shut off the lantern and poked his head out. He set the lantern on the other side of a brush pile and crawled up and over. Albert followed suit and looked around like a beaver peeking out of his den. A deep gully stretched before them and just around the bend spanned a small bridge.

"In the spring, I imagine this gulley's full of water," Elijah said. He spit and pointed. "Probably why these big branches are pushed against the hole."

"What's that up there?" Albert pointed toward a pile of rubbish and ripped sheets hanging from the bridge girders. They looked like curtains draped from the cross beams to the ground. Junk littered the area, such as: old tires, car parts, even the rusty shell of a wrecked Model A buried halfway up the doors.

"Hopefully, that there is Ol' Zephaniah. Now come on. We gots to be careful."

Albert stepped over the brush pile and sloshed through the gully. A greenish-brown mud covered them like paint and it smelled acrid. Albert's overalls grew stiff from the muck, and Elijah's shirt and trousers were as dark as his skin. Trees towered over the ditch, some reaching across to form a forest tunnel. The birds sang and a squirrel scampered through the roots of a tree that hung on the edge of the eroded ditch.

"Missed a rabbit and look where I am," Albert mumbled under his breath.

It was eerie and quiet like a forgotten woodland cemetery. The boys edged closer to the bridge, and Albert caught a glimpse through the sheets as they ruffled in a warm breeze. Where the girders and ground met, bricks had been laid for support. A small area had been leveled and constructed like a little room. Something hung from the girders that rattled like wind chimes, and a stained mattress rested on the uneven ground.

"Hey! You up there?" Elijah yelled. His voice reverberated off the concrete. Some leaves rustled. "We needin' our fortunes told."

Elijah motioned to Albert, and they crept up the gully's steep sides. They stood directly below the curtained "room," and Elijah pulled back one edge of the sheet. They heard a rustle followed by a grunt. Just on the other side of the mattress, dust blew out of a large hole below the bricks, like there was a burrow of some sort.

"Elijah, I don't think we should be here."

Elijah shook his head. The slapdash dwelling was empty except for the rustling and grunting in the hole.

"Zephaniah ain't here—"

A squeal pierced their ears, and a hairy black ball shot from the hole. Albert dove out of the way, and the creature ran over Elijah, knocking him backwards out of the sheets and down the hill. It stomped and charged and squealed over Elijah's screams, ramming him with its head, rolling him down the sides of the ditch and back into the water.

An arm wrapped around Albert's throat, and a dark hand poked a knife against his cheek. Albert's heart seemed to leap in his throat, and breath was not to be had. Matted ropes of black hair bounced on his shoulder, and a stringy beard tickled his ear. The captor giggled and whispered, "Thieves get deys throat cut, boy."

Chapter Four

Albert whimpered as the blade grazed his cheek. All the while, his captor laughed at Elijah having been toppled down the hill.

"We got money!" Elijah yelled between pig squeals and grunts.

"Money?" the man repeated. "Hmmm. Money is good," he said and loosened his grip from Albert's neck.

The man's dark, scar-covered arm stunk with sweat and filth. Albert felt the man's matted beard move when he spoke. "I like me some money," he said in a deep throaty voice that sounded more like a growl.

"Mojo!" he yelled. "Pa kounye!"

The little boar withdrew the attack and turned his tail toward Elijah, kicking dirt as if covering his excrement. Then, up the hill he trotted past Albert, snorting as he entered the curtains, rustling around on the dirty mattress. Elijah lie in the grass, recovering from the swine's vicious attack.

"You be lucky that Mojo dropped his tusks," the man giggled, "cause he'd have sliced you to ribbons if he had made use of 'em."

Elijah rolled over and pushed himself up. Grass and dirt tangled in his hair. He stormed up the hill. The man let loose of Albert and shoved him toward his approaching partner.

"Devil pig! Gonna be bacon if he touches me again!" Elijah pointed toward the dark hole.

Zephaniah was unlike anyone Albert had ever seen. He was dark as the night except for white bloodshot eyes. Long matted strands of hair puffed from his head and hung like tentacles past his shoulders. Caked with mud and flecked with grey, his patchy beard dangled from his chin. A dusty shirt clung to him by a single button, and his pants were cinched tight by a rope. A necklace of bones draped around his neck.

"What's wrong, Whitey, ain't you seen a voodoo priest?" Reaching in his pocket, he pulled out a stick topped with a squirrel skull, like a morbid lolly-pop, and shook it in Albert's face. It rattled, and the witch doctor mouthed "Boo" and laughed deep from his chest.

Albert winced and turned his head as Zephaniah cackled and whooped.

"Scared of Zephaniah and Mojo? Should be, oh, you should be messin' yourselves. Why are two boys spying my tent?"

Elijah took a deep breath and said, "We found something and need answers. My Pap told me that you know about anything and everything that happens in the city."

"What's yo Pap's name?"

"Robert Smith Jones."

"Lives in the Shanties? Met him once—wouldn't have nut'in to do with me," he said and stared at Elijah, looking right into his eyes, smiling. "Smart man."

Elijah stared at the ground.

"I like yo pap. He's good. Why ain't you asking yo pap what you be need'in to know?"

Elijah continued to stare. Albert did not know what to say except that he wished he had not come on this infernal treasure hunt. The desire to run washed over him like it had done so many times since they had first started the journey.

"You're doin' something he'd tan you for, ain't ya?"

Zephaniah grunted then turned to Albert whose heart was pounding and sweat was pouring from his forehead. Zephaniah was wild, untamable, and he had Albert cornered.

"What happened to you, Whitey?" His long finger pointed at Albert's face. "Got in a cat fight?"

Albert lowered his head. There was nowhere to go.

"How does a big boy like you get whipped? Answer, boy!"

"I...I don't..."

"Coward? I can sees the yella in ya."

It was like being naked before the whole world. Albert wished he were dead, wished he had drowned the fateful night Pete lost his mind.

"We got two dollars and a map. Can you take a look?" Elijah interrupted.

Zephaniah turned his attention back to Elijah and said, "What a minute: you that boy named Elijah who does all that preachin'?"

Albert looked up from his shame.

"Yep."

A smile broke across Zephaniah's face, and then he bellowed a hearty laugh. "I hear you preach and teach the bugs ev'n if nobody listens."

"Practicin'," Elijah said.

"Hand me yo money," Zephaniah shook his head, "come on." The voodoo priest turned and entered the bridge tent.

Filing in behind Elijah, Albert entered another world where the only comforting thing was the sunlight that peeked through the ripped curtains. Two pin-poke dolls huddled among some candles in the corner. A macabre chandelier of animal bones hung from little strings tied to the girder bolts, and they made a hollow tinking noise above their heads. Two springs protruded from a stained mattress, and beside the bed, a circle of stones acted as a fire pit for cooking. The two boys and the witch doctor hunched down in the make-shift room. Mojo grunted from inside his burrow.

Elijah handed the sewer map to Zephaniah who reached in his frayed shirt pocket for his glasses. A lens was missing in one rim and the other was cracked across the middle. He stared, bringing the paper to his face, turning it over, then repeating the process.

"Whatcha see?" Elijah asked.

"I see the name of a bootlegger: George Kelly Barnes. 'Machine Gun' is what that crazy wife called him."

"Didn't he rob banks?" Elijah asked.

"Yep, and he kidnapped a guy for ransom. He left these parts for a while, and then da fool returned. He be doin' all sorts of secret things, hangin' round the river, and by-god got himself arrested. The police never recovered all the money they say he had on him."

Elijah looked at Albert.

"They snooped all parts and questioned all sorts of folks but finally gave up."

"You think it's hidden somewhere?"

"Maybe, or it mighta been just a story. Some say that he hid da money on Mud Island or another sand bar. Others say he found a spot deep under the city. People make up tales all the time." Zephaniah then spotted something on the map. "Now that's interestin'. You see the letters there?"

Elijah leaned over. Albert wanted to see, but he kept his distance.

"That looks like an 'FS'. Whose map is dis?"

"Mine. I found it," Elijah answered.

"Where?"

"In the sewers."

"This FS musta lost it because his initials is written at the top right. So you just found it layin' round?"

Elijah didn't answer.

"I see. You got this in some way that you don't want nobody to know 'bout. Well, if this is what I think, and the stories is true, then FS is gonna want it back. What about you, white boy? What's your place here?"

Albert's eyes widened. Elijah stared at him as if screaming to stay quiet.

"Com'on, boy, speak!"

Albert stammered: "I'm here to help Elijah."

Zephaniah stared deep into his eyes, like he spotted something floating around in his eyeballs. His brow furrowed, then softened, then he laughed. Albert had a strange feeling that Zephaniah now knew something about him that no one else knew—that he had discovered his secret.

"Elijah, I ain't never met a Negro who had him a white slave, but it seems you do! " Zephaniah shook his head and continued to giggle while he reached under the mattress and pulled out a dented tin plate.

Albert was embarrassed and ashamed; a soft sheep was all he heard. But his shame turned to curiosity when Zephaniah pulled down some dangling bones and placed them in the pan. He sprinkled them with some powder from a leather pouch that hung on his bone necklace. Placing the map on top, he mumbled some phrases in the strange language that he had hollered earlier at Mojo.

Slipping out a knife, he seized Albert's hand. Albert went to jerk away, but it seemed useless against the old Haitian. The veins bulged from his arms as he yanked Albert close. Albert squirmed, and his screams froze in his throat. He could not wrench his arms from the grip. Zephaniah held Albert's hand across his leg and pressed the blade toward his fingers. The jagged blade looked as if it could slice through flesh like butter.

Albert's flesh!

Zephaniah was going to chop his fingers off and add them to his collection! Albert whined and blubbered, "No, Please!"

Elijah stood, "Let him go!"

"MOJO!"

There was a rustle and the boar appeared from his hole and stood at alert. Elijah froze.

Zephaniah pressed the knife until it parted the skin of Albert's index finger. His warm blood ran and pooled in the plate. Albert grunted and moaned at the burn of the jagged blade.

Zephaniah let go, and Albert recoiled and gripped his fingers tight, tears filling his eyes. Zephaniah ignored him.

Humming and mumbling, Zephaniah tossed the bones in the pan. Albert forgot his throbbing finger and looked to Elijah for an answer, but the little preacher was dumbstruck. Zephaniah rocked back and forth and moved his lips, muttering. It was like a song, but instead of words, he blabbered, "Inwit aaa mazzditaa oowta de hoooondwahh," repeating the foreign sounds over and over, faster and faster, louder and louder, and then he stopped and sat perfectly straight and still. Eyes closed, trancelike, he spoke in his deep froggy voice:

> In da deep water night,
> Below da suzie and drake,
> Lies a giant, a fight,
> A chief must awake,
> Finding hope and light.

Snapping his eyes open, there was nothing but the whites. He shook and groaned louder and louder; spit foamed in the corners of his mouth and ran down his beard. Mojo whimpered and retreated to his lair.

Elijah looked at Albert—a signal to make a run for it. Albert jumped up and Elijah grabbed the map from the plate, knocking the bones and blood all over the ripped mattress and grass. They scrambled out of the viaduct, Zephaniah still moaning on his mattress. They jumped to the bottom of the gully and sprinted to the sewers.

"Rete! MOJO! Prese, Prese!" echoed behind them. Albert turned and saw the black boar tearing down the embankment, splashing into the gully after them.

"Hurry, Elijah!"

The pipe opening was just yards away. Elijah streaked ahead of Albert, his bare feet splashing the pooled ditch water. Albert heard the squeals of the pig. Elijah reached the mouth, grabbed the lantern, and squeezed over through the brush. He turned and motioned for Albert to hurry.

"Don't quit Albert!"

The pig closed in on them, grunting with every stride. Albert pushed his legs to go faster. The animal squealed, right on his heels, his snout just inches away. Any closer and he would take a dive at Albert's legs.

Elijah hollered and cheered Albert toward the sewer opening. Gasping and crying, Albert jumped at the last possible moment and crashed through the top of the brush opening that covered the hole. It was the perfect dive, and he slipped right into the pipe mouth, scraping only his back against the top. The little boar slammed into the thick, thorny branches and squealed, fighting to get through.

Albert had scrapes down his chest, and his back felt raw. Mojo shrieked in the tangles; the childlike screams echoed through the pipes as Albert scooted in the dark. Elijah waited for him and huddled in the silt, cursing the pig, pronouncing his intentions of making him bacon at their next encounter.

Chapter Five

The boar gave up, grunted, and returned to Zephaniah.

"Give us a light, Albert."

He fumbled in his front pocket for the matchbox and handed it to Elijah.

"They is wet."

Albert reached around to feel the scrapes on his back.

"Sorry. They must've got soaked when I dove."

Elijah looked down, his mouth moved either in prayer or disdain.

The Zippo. Albert had almost forgotten. He grabbed it and started flicking. There were sparks and then a muted flame. Elijah raised his head, eyes wide in the light. He grabbed the lantern and lifted the mud-splashed glass. Albert lit the wick and it glowed.

"Let yo light shine for the world. Great job, Albert." He slapped him on the shoulder and clapped like he was in church. "Now, let's do some figurin'. That craziness is a good hint that this is a map to Kelly's treasure. Did you hear his prophecy?"

"Yeah, what was that? What's a Suzie and Drake? I mean, I know they are ducks, but where do you think we got to find ducks?

"Aside from swimmin' in the river, I gots no idea."

"And what happened to his eyes and all the moaning?" Albert found the worst of the scraped skin on his back and he winced.

"Zephaniah is a bona fide voodoo priest. He was talkin' through the spirits of the bones. They tell him what can't be seen. He said 'in the dark and deep, beneath a suzie and drake lies *hope*.' I believes with all my heart that is the treasure. We are in the dark and deep right now!" He unfolded the map and pointed his skinny finger along the lines. "We's right here, and it looks like the FS fella has been all around here from those marks."

Albert saw a cluster of little x's like systematic check-offs. If the marks coincided with the marks in the sewer, then FS was marking off each section of sewer as he explored.

"My guess is: FS lost this map before he was able to search this here area." Elijah pointed to a large space where the grid had not been marked. It looked like several miles of sewer walk to Albert. "I think we should look here, where there ain't no marks."

"You think we'll run into him?"

"FS? Well, maybe, but remember: we got his map and he's not going to get far without it. Now, we need to be a headin' down this tunnel, going that way." Elijah started scooting through the pipe. The water echoed again through the darkness.

Albert was already lost, and his mind ran to the other part of the oracle, the part that scared him. "What about the giant and fight?"

"Albert, I know you is scared. I saw you bow yo head up there, and I thought you'd run."

"I nearly did."

"But, I knows you have it in you."

"What? What's in me?"

Elijah stopped moving forward. He turned, lifted the lantern up to his face, and he looked straight into Albert's eyes.

"Potential. Courage," Elijah said, pointing at Albert's chest. "It's in there, way deep. Jus' gotta dig it up, that's all. Look at what all you done already. You've faced a wild pig and a foaming mouthed voodoo man. Ain't many say they did that."

Albert did not know what to say. Elijah turned and plodded ahead then glanced back again.

"You's gonna realize yo power one day, and 'Katie, bar the door' when you do. Now, come on. We's got to find this suzie and drake or whatever it is."

Albert followed. His stomach rumbled, and he realized he had not eaten all day. Rats scurried around the pipes—more than he had seen so far. If he could eat rat, he would be a fat man.

Elijah sloshed a few yards and stopped and peered at the map. This went on over and over: slosh, stop, look, slosh, stop, look. Typically, when they stopped, it meant a turn down some new pipe. It was a maze of the worst kind—a giant, dark, watery maze where they raced with rats and roaches by the hundreds.

"Hey, Elijah, um...why isn't there poop in here?"

"Whatcha think you is walkin' on?"

Albert felt himself getting sick.

"Oh, I's just jokin'. The sewer is divided into storm and sanitation. Keeps from disease. We in the storm sewer, but, you start seein' some turds, you holler 'cause dat means it's flooding."

Elijah stopped and stared at a pipe that was smaller than the one they were in currently.

"We got to cross through here."

It was small and would be tight. Albert had never been in such confined spaces, and now it was getting even tighter, and the water would close in around him. His neck grew hot. Then he saw something on the pipe above the small opening resembling two chalk letters.

"Elijah," he said and pointed.

Elijah lifted the light to see a scratchy FS looming over the opening.

"That's…"

"I know. We be followin' him."

Albert's heart thumped in his chest. He did not have a good feeling about this FS. Elijah had found the map on a dead body—a map to rumored lost ransom money of a notorious bank robber. FS was probably not a person he would want to encounter, and since there were still many areas left unchecked, FS probably wanted his map back. And here they were in a dark maze where he could lurk around any corner.

Albert felt lightheaded and broke a cold sweat. Only the thoughts of family, the rifle, and his chance to make everything okay kept him from fleeing. Then there were Elijah's words—probably the best words he had ever listened to in all his life. Elijah saw something in him, and nobody had been able to do that.

Elijah volunteered to go first. He placed the lantern in the hole and scrunched down with it, worming his way inside the pipe. Once his feet disappeared, it was Albert's turn, and he was about to throw up from nerves. Tight spots were not what he enjoyed, and being a big boy meant he would probably never get unstuck. Nevertheless, he took a deep breath and crawled in, pulling with his arms and squirming his body.

It was the darkest dark he had ever seen. Water rose up to his chin, and he could not see his hands as he pulled himself along the bottom. He breathed harder. The sounds of his huffing reverberated in his ears. What if water rushed around him? There would be no way out. It would be a wet coffin. He grunted and panted and pulled faster, pushing with his feet. The pipe was tight and solid, and it squeezed him like a python. As he scooted in the muck, it stirred up a rotten egg-like stink and he gagged.

Elijah's light glowed ahead, and Albert breathed a little easier.

"Rats!" Elijah echoed as he reached the end of the chute and crawled out. He poked his head back into the hole. "Albert, when you come out, you be careful to stay on the ledge."

A noise grew, like the crowd at a stadium, but as Albert neared the opening and listened, the sounds of cheering twisted to squeals and shrieks. He could barely think over the chatter. He poked his head out of the pipe and saw Elijah standing to his left on a ledge, just wide enough for his bare feet. Elijah held the lantern out, revealing a round room. The ledge circled around the wall to another chute on the other side. The squeals pierced Albert's ears, and it looked like the walls and pit below were moving.

The pit, the walls, the ledge—everywhere—crawled with rats.

The round room looked like a bowl of living rat soup. They scrambled along the ledges—big, fat, gray ones with long whip-like tails, skinny brown rats whose ribs shown from lack of food. They crept, sniffed, bit, nuzzled, and ran all over the tops of one another, the weak ones devoured by the strong. Above, like a chandelier in a dining hall, hung a large pipe and spout. It looked like the spout of a kitchen sink, a giant sink filled with rodents.

"Albert, be careful," Elijah yelled. "We gotta walk the ledge to get to that tunnel opposite here. We slip and the starvin' ones will have dinner. "

It was time to run. No way could he walk the ledge, but there was nowhere to go. He would be lost in the sewers, and Elijah was already halfway across. There was no choice but to risk it and push forward.

He edged out of the pipe and balanced on the ledge. Rats scampered all around his feet. Another dropped down his overalls and nuzzled along his leg. He shook and kicked it out while another crawled around his neck, its wet nose sniffed his ear; its claws scratched his skin as it dug in for balance. But Albert could only focus on his task at hand, and he clinched his toes in his water-logged shoes forcing the soles around the concrete.

Elijah had his own war to wage, fighting to get a black rat off his shoulder with his free arm. He could not swing the lantern around to scrape it.

"It's biting me!" he yelled as he slammed his back hard against the wall, toppling a little. Albert reached out to steady him. The injured rat squealed and careened off the ledge into the pit to be torn to pieces by the healthy.

The one on Albert's neck crawled down his back and nibbled on his underwear. Albert yelled and slapped behind him, losing his balance. He twisted and slipped and bounced his butt on the ledge. Elijah caught his arm as he fell, and Albert grabbed the lip of concrete with his other hand.

"Hold on, Al!"

Rats clawed and nibbled at his ankles. Their sharp teeth dug into his calf, and Albert panicked, kicking and swinging and rubbing his legs together, anything to get them off. He held onto the ledge and squeezed Elijah's hand and pulled himself up. It was too close of a call. The rats squealed and churned louder.

"We got to get outta here before that happens ag'in," Elijah shouted.

Albert scooted his feet, whimpering, his chest and face pressed against the wall, feet bull-dozing rats from the ledge. Elijah lead the way around the shelf, shuffling his feet. Albert forced himself to look ahead to the tunnel but could not help peeking down at the churning wave of rodents. They swirled and gurgled like the eddies in the muddy Mississippi.

"Hold da lantern," Elijah said, having reached the opening.

Albert grabbed the light, and Elijah slipped down the wall and disappeared into the mouth.

Poking his head out, he reached for the lantern, then disappeared again. Albert scooted over and slid down on his knees and plunged into the hole. He crawled and followed the bobbing light. Tears welled up in his eyes. He was nearly torn apart. Pausing, he leaned to catch his breath. There had been too many of these close calls.

"Come on Albert!" Elijah motioned at him and then turned down another pipe. But Albert sat for a while longer. He needed a minute. Then he forced himself to his knees and lurched along until Elijah screamed.

Albert scrambled down the pipe and turned down the one where Elijah had ventured. His screams silenced. The pipe widened enough for Albert to stand, and he sloshed toward the light. Rot filled the air so that he nearly puked. Elijah squatted next to a big pile, his hands covering his mouth. It was a bulging man; his swollen blue fingers hung out from his layers of clothes.

"Sweet Jesus! Another body," Elijah said, "cut in the throat jus' like the last one."

Large chunks were missing from his contorted face, presumably from rat bites. Albert turned and gagged. He had seen death once before, and it still haunted his dreams.

"We gotta get out of here, Elijah," he said, wiping his mouth.

"Hold on another minute."

A rat squirmed from the corpse's pant leg. Elijah searched the man's pockets but found nothing. He lifted the lantern, casting light on the wall above the body. Albert knew what would be there, and just as he thought, scratched above the body like an epitaph was another FS.

It was too much. The hunt for treasure had become a race with a killer.

"Elijah," Albert said, "I think..."

A clank and a whooshing sound echoed from the tunnel they had exited. A gaggle of squeals filled the air. Rats poured down the pipe, washing around the boys and running into the darkness. They screeched and darted, not stopping to pick at the dead body; then a roar and a splash followed.

Albert froze and panicked but then felt a new coolness on his feet and his ankles. Water rose quickly.

"Follow dem rats!" Elijah yelled.

A wave rushed into their pipe slamming both of the boys down. The lantern popped and everything went black. Albert fought to swim as the water shoved him along, rising over his head. It filled his nose and mouth as he coughed and gasped. He bounced and rolled and shot through the pipe, barely gulping air, fighting through swimming rodents. He finally took a breath but smashed his head on the top of the concrete sewer. His lungs burned as he twisted and turned, chasing his air supply along the shifting sewer.

This is what drowning felt like: a violent invasion of liquid, a siege of air.

He felt a tugging on his overall strap and a yank, and he broke the surface. Rats flopped past him in the rapids. He coughed and vomited in the passing water and spotted a sparkle above him.

Chapter Six

"Grab da ladder! I can't hold you long!"

Metal rungs protruded from the concrete. Albert grabbed one and felt Elijah release. The water still rushing under them, Albert stumbled up the tiny treads. They had found a manhole.

"Thanks," Albert rasped, "again."

"Lucky, that's all. Just reached for whatever I could. I almos' let ya slip."

"What happened?" Albert said, gagging and coughing some more.

"Somebody done turn on the flush tank. That huge hanging pipe back there filled up the rat tank and flushed out any clogs in the sewer. Guess it worked."

Elijah felt around his shirt; he dug down into his pockets. "Oh, no," he felt all over his pants, "it's gone! The map, it's gone!" Elijah hung there on the ladder, worry washing over him like the water in the pipe.

"What do we do? How are we gonna find the treasure without the map?"

"I don't know," Elijah said, staring past Albert. Something big was going through his head. "We got an oracle though, Albert, an oracle that says it's below a suzie and drake. What was the rest?"

"There's a giant and a fight and the rising of a chief and hope—the chief rises and there is hope."

Elijah's eyes brightened. "I know: no matter what, we got to keep at it. Between the oracle, two dead bodies, the map, and this FS fella, I'm convinced that there's something to the rumors. We jus' gotta find some ducks... a drake and suzie. But we need another lantern or something to light our way."

Elijah looked around in the faint light from the keyhole in the manhole cover above, then he looked below again. "I bet they is a ton of change now after all that there washin'."

Albert's face lit up, and he reached into his pocket. The zippo lighter was still there and was actually cleaner than when he had first found it. He pulled it out, flipped the top, and ripped his thumb along the wheel. Hopefully, the water had not harmed it. The wheel spun and sparked and then emitted a flame.

"Let's get to looking then," he said, but he spoke with something new: confidence. He had felt it long ago, often when he was fishing with Pete, but it had been torn from him. He hopped down into the trickling water; the fresh silt squished under his soaked shoes.

Elijah reached bottom, and Albert flicked the light again. It was a small fire but a glow big enough to reveal the junk that scattered and studded like patches of clover. The boys prodded and picked through clods of rotten leaves, cigarette butts, and the occasional tin can. The flame burned Albert's hand, but he felt useful. He switched the lighter from hand to hand to relieve the pain.

Despite losing the map, he was convinced they could actually find the treasure. However, the body they discovered scared him. It was another murder, a sure sign that they were closing in on something valuable.

Maybe it was Elijah's confidence or maybe it was their successful navigation through adventure, but he felt alive digging and picking coins.

"How much you think you got?"

Albert squinted in the flicker of the flame and said, "Maybe a dollar or two."

"Same here. Let's go up and see if we can finds us a store."

With the change in their pockets, the two boys climbed the rungs up the manhole.

"Albert, we need you to pop the lid."

Albert slipped by and pulled himself above Elijah. He braced his hands on the cover. Tires roared and whished overhead. He pushed and the cover shifted slightly. Bracing his arms again, he pressed hard so that his body shook and the seal broke and light entered. After another whish, he slid the lid up and out, onto the concrete road.

Albert lifted his head into the sunlight to hazard a glance, then ducked; a car horn blared as the undercarriage zipped overhead. Then he chanced it again.

A truck idled at an intersection in the distance, far enough away that Albert had time to climb up and yank Elijah out with him. They slid the cover back in place and ran toward the cracked sidewalk. The welcomed sunlight forced them to squint, and a wonderful aroma filled Albert's nose: smoked meat.

"I hear music, the Blues. You?" asked Elijah.

"I smell barbeque."

"Oh, yeah, just what I thought. We be close to Beale, W.C. Handy's ole' stompin' ground. Follow me, Albert, and hopefully we'll snag some food and find a light."

They turned down a busy intersection and crossed another street and approached a smaller cobblestone road buzzing with music. The afternoon sun beat down on the buildings, throwing their shadows upon the paths and patrons. Huge signs with unlit lights dangled overhead. One read: "Hotel Clark, The Best Service for Colored Only." Three black men, sweat staining their shirts, sloped on either side of the entrance. Their eyes followed Albert as he walked with

Elijah, but they were easy to forget when the sweet, smoky, pork smell rushed his nose. His stomach growled and clawed.

Some fat men across the street tended long barrels, smoke twisting out of the small stovepipes that stood on their tops. They opened the lids and a cloud rolled out and dissipated, revealing slabs of sizzling ribs. Humming approval, they slathered the meat with sauce, their eyes red from long hours smoldering hickory.

It was a carnival of food and fun. Men and women chatted while others danced to the minstrels' strumming guitars. Trumpeters, their cheeks pregnant with air, blew shrilly in the afternoon air.

Elijah pointed and said, "That's where we be needin' to go."

A glass-fronted, two-story building leaned between the others. Hanging over the door was a black sign that read: A. Schwab, established 1876.

"My daddy told me 'bout this place. He say it is a cornucopia of anything you want," Elijah said.

The boys crossed the street and turned into the store. A bell tinkled and the wood floors creaked when they entered. Their eyes darted around the mountains of bins and rows of shelves filled with everything from beans, to hammers, to candy. The candy was an oasis in the middle of junky tools. Glass jars of jawbreakers and long lollipops towered over licorice bins and boxes of chocolates and Cracker Jacks. In the back corner, a rickety staircase bent and twisted; mule harnesses and farming implements lined the sides leaving a small trail up the center. Climbing to the upper floors would be a feat for only the bravest junk hunters.

"If we don't find treasure, we should come back here," Albert whispered.

Elijah did not answer. He just stood still, mesmerized. Someone, however, caught Albert's attention. Regardless of all the crazy items that would command the attention of any boy, the most interesting thing to him was a fidgety, red-headed man squabbling with the clerk.

"Can I get store credit? I'm good for it, I tell ya."

His accent matched his father's, just a bit thicker. He must have immigrated recently. A derby-style hat, speckled in mud, pressed his red curls around his ears. Little round spectacles slid down his nose when he talked, and he constantly pushed them back into place. Leaning on a shovel, he fidgeted and folded a dirty, torn piece of paper with his free hand. He stared at the paper and sat down the shovel and folded the paper over and over as the clerk called to someone in a back room. Pulling out a pocket watch, he cleared his throat and looked at the map again.

"Here's an old lantern, gots some oil in it!" Elijah said. "Cost three dollars."

An argument ensued, one demanding credit and the other refusing. There was something interesting about the red-headed man, his constant fidgeting and fingering of the paper–folded, unfolded, in pocket, out of pocket. It was if the paper had become a part of him–a talisman of sorts. His face grew as red as his hair.

"We got just a'nuf for Moon Pies. Want one?" Elijah asked.

"Huh?" said Albert. "Oh...yeah, I'm starving."

The boys went up to the counter.

"I need this credit!" The man slammed his hand on the counter. "I'll pay as soon as I hit the mother-load!"

"I think it's time for you to leave, Mister," the owner said, appearing from the back of the store, "before I call the police."

The man grit his teeth, grabbed his paper, and pointed a dirty finger at the storeowner saying, "Remember this moment you refused me; remember so you will not cry *injustice*." He said it like an ancient prophet warning of impending doom.

The paper flopped open in his hand and Albert's stomach dropped. Scrawled marks filled a grid, like the marks on their map. The man spun to leave but then stopped and stared at the tarnished coins Elijah piled on the counter. Up and down at the boys he gazed and slid his round spectacles up his nose.

He looked like a starving wolf, staring and licking his chops. Then he turned and bumped into a carousel of postcards that almost toppled had he not caught one of the shelves. He bent down and picked up the handful that fell.

Elijah counted the money while Albert kept watch on the man who eyed back at them, hands fidgeting with the paper in between shuffling the cards. They grabbed the lantern and rushed by him and out the door. Albert opened his moon pie and took a bite.

"Is he followin' us?" mumbled Elijah between bites.

Albert turned and saw no one.

"No. Did you see his paper?"

"Yep, it was our map's partner."

Albert felt like a deer crossing an open field. They were being watched, but he tried to convince himself that it must be all the people on Beale. They passed a few clubs that were starting to awaken in the late afternoon. A man sprawled on the sidewalk plucking a guitar, running his hand up and down the neck with a metal tube he would answer its whines with a raspy few lines of his own creation.

The moon pies had barely touched their hunger, and a corner barbeque joint drew them close. Flies swarmed a lone sandwich that sat on an empty outside table. It dripped in sweet brown sauce and creamy coleslaw. Mesmerized by the sandwich, they bumped right into a man who grabbed Elijah's wrist and squeezed tight. It was the man from the store.

"Sorry, sir."

"Where you goin' with the lantern?"

Elijah yanked his arm to no avail and said, "We's goin' catfishin' tonight, sir, runnin' trotlines on the river."

The red-headed man let go and pushed his glasses up his nose. He grabbed the barbeque sandwich off the plate and took a bite. Chunks fell out of his mouth as he mumbled, "I noticed all the change you used to pay for it. Where'd that come from?"

"We's found it. It's ours. Now, we gotta go 'foe we misses the best fishin'."

The man leaned close and hissed, "What are you doin' in the sewers?" He smacked as he interrogated.

"Not sure what you're talking 'bout, but we is going now," Elijah answered and forced past the man, only to be yanked back by him.

The man wrapped the sandwich and stuffed it in his pocket.

"Not so fast, Blackie; I think you're pretty familiar with the sewers, and I think I could use some helpers. Can't get good help, lately...had to show some of my employees a little... *justice*."

He swung them around and forced them down the street. "Unless you want your gullets opened, you'll come along quietly."

Albert fought to free his arm. Elijah's eyes widened, darting around, looking for help.

"Hey Red! Hold it right there!"

Albert turned to see a police officer stalking, his hand on the club at his waist.

"You the one causing trouble at Schwabs?"

"A little misunderstanding of credit, Officer, between me and the owner."

"You pay for that sandwich? Or you just get it on credit?" He pointed at the wrapper that hung out of his trouser pocket.

The man let go of their arms. Elijah took one look at Albert, and they darted down the street.

"Hey! Come back here!" the officer yelled, but nothing would stop them. They turned down Second

Street, cars lined from bumper to bumper, then they crossed an alley and dodged a delivery truck.

Albert's heart thumped out of his chest. They turned right down another alley and then left again along another busy street, sidestepping and weaving through the crowds. Cars roared and stopped, horns honked, a taxi driver yelled something out of his window, and Albert did all he could to keep up. Elijah had boundless energy and did not seem to slow, but Albert was a big boy, and his size slowed him down.

They turned up another street and stopped in front of a brown ornate building. Red canvas awnings topped every window and door, and a black man waited outside in a dark suit. A red, round, brimless hat perched on top of his bald head. People strolled up, and the man opened the door, grabbing their suitcases to carry inside. Albert read the copper plate on the side of the entrance: The Peabody.

"I think we's clear," Elijah huffed.

"Think we should hide in there? Just in case," Albert said huffing, leaning over as a pain shot through his side.

"Shoo! Look at us! We look like a dog buried us and then dug us up three days later, and I ain't wearin' one of them suits like that fella. You think they gonna let me in?" Elijah asked. "I'd love to sneaks in there though. Hear they got some ducks swimmin' in a fountain."

The boys still fought to catch their breath and then stared at one another.

"Did you say ducks?" Albert asked.

"Yeah... I did." Elijah stared at the building and mumbled, "Some drunk fellas did it as a joke. You think...?"

"The oracle: 'Beneath the suzie and drake...'"

"Sweet Lord! We found it! Of course. The Peabody. It's beneath this hotel. Kelly wanted to be like all them other gangsters, hiding around fine hotels."

Elijah looked around the street between rushing cars and found a manhole. "Ready to go?"

"I've never been more ready." Albert smiled and the boys stepped into the street and stood over a cover. Albert wiggled his fingers in the hole and yanked. The cover held and then the creviced dirt broke loose. A car squealed before them and honked; people along the street pointed, shocked at two boys who seemed to go where they pleased. Albert slid the cover over, and the two boys climbed into the void and disappeared, dropping down into the dark.

Chapter Seven

Elijah stood at the bottom of the ladder and lit the lantern while Albert slid the cover back over the man hole. Soft light ran down the pipes.

This section of sewer was very old. Instead of smooth concrete, the walls were brick and mortar. Slimy algae crawled along the sides, and the normal residents, cockroaches, scanned the invaders with their oscillating antennae. It smelled old and musty, like an uninhabited house, and if it were possible, it felt darker. Cobwebs stretched across everything like transparent sheets.

"This sewer musta been 'round when the Yellow Fever was ragin'," Elijah said, handing the Zippo back then sloshing around, feeling the walls. "Look real close, Albert. Look for anything that you could hide money in."

Albert had to stoop slightly in this particular pipe. The brick had been slathered in places by an overabundance of mortar, probably a patch for holes, giving the appearance of stone. Dripping echoed off the brick, and the odor of rotten eggs became more pungent the deeper they ventured. Albert searched and even dug down in the silt. He dreamed of toting home bags of money, bulging bags with dollar signs on them. His family would cheer with Albert standing in the doorway lifting the bags like Pete had done with the catfish.

"Elijah, what are you going to do with your half?"

Elijah smiled. "Gonna get me some new clothes, that's for sure. After that, books for my Pap."

Albert followed as they turned down another pipe. "How did you get so smart anyway? You said you don't go to school much."

"Momma died when I's born, so Paps took up the slack. He got lucky and found a janitor job at the teacher college. He works at night. One of dem professors stayed late every day and decided he was gonna teach Pap to read and write. So, Pap brought home the books and learned his letters. I wanted to be like Pap so..."

"You learned to read."

Elijah lifted the lantern and peered down into a dark chute. He motioned for Albert to follow. "Yep, I read everythin' I could get my hands on: Homer, Plato, Dickens, you name it. Paps wasn't gonna waste any chance for my learnin'. Sent me to school and I was there for three days."

"Why only three?"

"They kicked me out 'cause I corrected they's mistakes. Crazy lady tryin' to say Aristotle was the greatest of all them phi-lo-so-phers. I told her he couldn't hold a light to Plato. He was the Moses of the Greeks, I tell ya."

"I never thought teachers were wrong."

"Oh, they is wrong a lot and don't take well to correcting. Man, she yanked me up and switched my hind parts until I say I was wrong."

"Did you say it?"

"Yep, told her I made a mistake, Socrates was better too!"

Albert laughed although he had no idea who the men were that Elijah was talking about, but he envisioned Elijah standing and aiming that bony finger, giving that teacher a review.

"Did you see that rat?" Elijah pointed.

"There are a ton of rats down here. Remember the swarm we nearly drowned with?"

Elijah moved deeper into the chute, but something captured his full attention. Albert grunted at the inconvenience because the passage was small, forcing him to crawl on hands and knees.

"Rats just keep appearing right there on the side of the pipe, right there. See? There goes another! Like he done popped right outta the wall."

Just as Elijah said it, a brown rodent seemed to come out of the brick, scampered around and disappeared again.

"Probably a crack or a loose mortar patch. You said it's an old sewer, Elijah."

"I got a feelin," Elijah said, inching closer. "Look! There's something attached."

Albert saw it. A plate of some kind, made of thick, heavy iron. They crept closer. He had not seen anything like this so far. It was about the width of his shoulders and was held in place by four big screws. It was orange with rust. A brick had cracked on the bottom of the plate, leaving a small opening for the rats to run in and out as they pleased.

"My daddy knew a fella that worked for da city. Sewer inspector. He'd come down here and check things out. Sometimes he'd hunt for change. That's where I got the idea to go explorin.' Then I found that body. Anyways, when there's a hole, they have to repair it, sometimes use a metal plate."

"Where do you think it goes?"

Elijah stared, spit, and then took his finger and pointed in the air and moved it across toward the plate, like he was drawing a line.

"I think that hole goes right under The Peabody."

Albert grabbed the edges of the plate with his fingertips and pushed. He hit the center with his hand, but nothing—only a low gong. He pushed and pulled until the tips of his fingers burned.

"Ain't no use, Albert. That thing ain't movin'. We gotta try another way."

Albert relaxed. Sweat dripped down his forehead.

An inch. The plate was just an inch thick, yet it stopped them cold. The quest felt impossible.

"Wait a cotton-pickin' minute," Elijah said. "I got me an idea." He started back down the pipe from where they had just come from, saying, "Come on Albert!"

Albert splashed behind him but struggled to keep up as Elijah went faster in excitement. He was like an inventor that had finally figured out a solution to a persistent failing idea. He reached the manhole and motioned for Albert to hurry.

"Looks like we got to find a way into that hotel after all."

Albert scrambled up the ladder. He pressed the cover and light rolled in like water. Sliding it over, he paused for cars to pass. An undercarriage rattled by, the tires roared and the brakes squeaked. He took a deep breath and attempted a peek. Traffic had cleared, so he hopped up and yanked Elijah into the light.

"Hey!! What are you boys doing in that sewer?"

He had not spotted the policeman on the corner across from the hotel, but the policeman did not miss them. He had been scribbling a parking ticket while a brown suited man protested his violation. He closed his pad and started toward them.

The boys bolted to the sidewalk and reached for the hotel door, but the doorman slid in front of the handle, blocking their entrance.

"You boys can't come in here."

"Hey! Stop them kids!" the policeman yelled as he weaved through screeching cars. One sped past and ran over the open manhole; its tire popped and then hissed, and it skidded to a stop.

"Please mister?" Elijah begged.

"Hold them there!" the policeman barked.

The driver of the car jumped out cussing, demanding to know who left the manhole uncovered.

"I can't let you in, boys."

They had to do something quick. Albert yanked on Elijah's shirt. "Let's go!" They sprinted around the corner.

"Stop!" someone yelled, but the voice faded as they ran. Elijah sprinted along the side of the hotel, and Albert followed until they reached a wrought-iron fence. They stopped, huffing and wheezing. The iron bars were painted the same brown as the hotel. Between the sections of fence stood brick columns. It was part of The Peabody, the parking lot. A loose chain dangled on the gate, padlocked. With the sun setting, shadows grew around the building and night neared. They needed to act quickly if they were going to get in.

"I gots an idea," Elijah said and pulled on the gates until the chain tightened and he squeezed through the gap. Once through, he pushed, stretching the chain as far as he could. Albert wedged his body through, but the iron pressed on his belly and chest. He started to panic thinking he was stuck, but he pushed hard and popped through.

The two boys scampered around the cars and squatted behind some shadowy bushes just shy of the hotel's valet entrance.

Two porters, wearing the same suit and round hat as the one in front, waited on a red carpet. A black sedan pulled up, and the taller of the two stepped to the rear door and opened it. A large white lady was scrunched in the back seat beside a man half her size. She fanned herself with a crimped church bulletin.

The scrawny man opened his side and sauntered around the car and opened the door. The porter reached for her hand, recoiled, and turned to walk inside the hotel. The scrawny man intervened and pulled the lady to her feet.

"I don't want some filthy negro to help me out of this car!" the woman barked. The other porter had darted inside and returned pushing a flat cart with brass arches on the ends. A brass bar stretched across the top connecting the arches.

"There's our Trojan horse," Elijah whispered. "Jus' gotta wait for the right moment."

Albert was not sure about a horse, but he figured they would be riding into the hotel in style. He waited for a signal. The porter circled the back of the car. The driver lumbered out and unlocked the trunk then returned to the wheel and ducked behind his newspaper, apparently knowing the drama that would ensue. The paper had large words like "Hitler" and "War," but Albert knew the driver was not really interested in reading, not with the lady causing a scene.

"And I don't want them preparing my food," she mouthed. "You are going to make sure of that, aren't you? Or do you even care for me?" she said and snatched her husband's handkerchief from his suit coat and bawled in it.

The porter hung some dresses on the brass rail. They nearly brushed the red velvet that lined the cart floor. Looking like small tents, Albert was sure he could fit two of himself in one dress.

"Darling, let's not make a scene," coaxed the husband.

The porter heaved two large suitcases from the trunk and slammed them on the cart.

"You don't love me! If you are not going to say anything, then I will!"

The woman shoved the man away and made for the door. The porter shot from the cart to the door to open it.

"Go!" Elijah whispered and the boys crept from the bushes to the cart and slid in between the suitcases. They crouched in the middle of the brass arches, and Albert yanked the hanging dresses around them like a curtain.

"Just get the bags, boy!" she yelled.

The porter grabbed the cart, his hands inches from Albert. It wobbled and then rolled. Albert grabbed Elijah to keep from toppling out.

"Man, that woman packs heaa-vy," the porter mumbled.

The cart stopped and a door opened. Elijah smiled. They were almost inside The Peabody. The wheels rocked over the threshold and rolled through the door and then through another. The sounds changed. There was no more dripping, or sloshing, or rotten egg smells. Talking and laughter echoed all around, and a piano tinkled in the background. Gurgling water filled the air.

The cart halted; Elijah motioned to Albert and they slid out from between the luggage. Albert had never seen such a place. Stone columns stretched high supporting a carved wooden ceiling. Massive chandeliers dangled from golden chains, spreading their decorative light on the marble floor that sparkled and stretched from wall to wall. A colorful area rug covered the marble floor in one area where couches and chairs were arranged like a large living room. Men in suits and women in dresses stood around sipping drinks from short glasses, chatting and laughing.

The gurgling came from a round fountain in the middle of the living room. A sprawling bouquet of flowers perched atop a towering bowl in the center. Water poured from the bowl into the surrounding pool.

Albert's heart leaped when he spotted a mallard duck, a drake, strutting his bright green head and quacking as he bobbed in the water. The suzie stood on a block and answered his call. The boys stood right in the middle of Zephaniah's oracle.

"Hey! You two! How'd you get in here?"

Albert turned and saw, on the far side of the bar, the porter who had denied them entrance. The porter stomped toward them.

Elijah grabbed Albert and said, "Split up! Go as low in the building as you can!" He shot off toward the elevators.

The porter broke into a run. Albert froze. Other porters and the bartender approached. He had never had trouble running before, but now his feet were in concrete. There were some stairs to the left that wound downward, and Albert broke into a sprint toward them.

"Stop that boy!" he heard as he reached the first step and jumped.

Chapter Eight

Albert slammed on the floor, barely landing on his feet. He turned down the next flight and took each step two at a time, racing as quickly as he could. Don't trip was all he could think. Hopefully, Elijah was able to distract the other pursuers.

Reaching the bottom, he looked down a large hallway lined with doors. At the end swung a double. Sizzles and yelling wafted through the hall, and he smelled fried chicken. He could almost taste the crispy, breaded, hot skin and the succulent meat. His stomach gurgled.

His pursuers were coming down the steps, so he made for the first door that opened. A lumberyard odor filled his nose, nothing like the wonderful hallway. His eyes adjusted to the dark, revealing a maze of various crates. There would be no better place to hide, so he shut the door behind him. The opaque window allowed only a pale light. He weaved among the crates and found a place to squat down and hide. Footsteps soon echoed down the hall, and two silhouettes appeared in front of the door. The doorknob turned, then light and noise poured into the room.

This was it. He would be caught and the quest would be over. He and Elijah were on the threshold of discovery, and it would soon be gone–a waste. Albert grit his teeth and thought about his family's brokenness when he returned home, and it would be even worse if his homecoming came by squad car.

Searching eyes scanned every box and corner, and he made himself as small as he could.

"What are you doing?"

They spotted him. He should make up something, an excuse of some sort. He started to get up.

"So, you are the ones who keep stealing wine from my closet," the same voice accused.

Albert froze. Stealing wine?

"We are looking for a vagrant, a kid," answered another voice.

"VAGRANT?" The first voice boomed, "GET OUT OF MY WINE BEFORE I HAVE YOUR JOBS! I DON'T CARE WHAT YOU ARE LOOKING FOR!"

The door slammed. The man yelled over the other two as they attempted an explanation. It must have been the chef, fed up with people sneaking food and drink from storage. Albert leaned against some crates and exhaled. That was too close. He had been a breath away from being captured. He needed Elijah, but he had no idea where he was or how they would reconnect.

What if he had been caught?

The thoughts were more than he could handle. He could not stay forever, but how long should he wait, and where would he go if Elijah never showed? Elijah had called the shots in this adventure. How could he make it without him? It would be impossible.

A small shadow scampered across the room, and then there was the sound of scratching. Albert squinted to see if he could spot the noise-maker. Fumbling around for his Zippo, he popped it open and ripped the wheel. The flame revealed a small rat, much like the ones he had seen in the sewers. The little fellow stared for a moment, sniffed around, and continued munching on a potato that he had swiped from the sack beside him–this was the storeroom raider.

Seeing the rat feasting made Albert's stomach rumble. The Moon Pie had only been a teaser, and the aroma of fried chicken was intoxicating. He looked around, found some bread, and ripped a corner. The porters would get into serious trouble if the chef found the mangled loaf. Albert looked around for his rodential partner-in-crime, but it had disappeared. Then he spotted a tail slipping into the floor.

"Follow dem rats," Elijah would say. That phrase was funny; everyone he had ever known hated rats, yet it was rats that had been their heroes. He had to investigate.

Tearing another hunk of bread, he scooted to where it disappeared. In the middle of the room was a large floor drain. The rat had wriggled through one of the wider spaces of the bent iron grates. Albert leaned his ear close. After a day in the sewers, the smell and sound was unmistakable. It must connect to the sewers, perhaps it was the other side of the blocked drainpipe?

He felt the grate. The bent bars not only allowed room enough for the hiding rat, but was large enough for him to reach through and grip. It looked heavy but not more than he could handle. He stuck the hunk of bread in his mouth and pulled for a little test.

It shifted.

A shadow appeared in the door window and the knob turned. The porters were back. They would search the room thoroughly this time. He had to move quickly.

He lifted the grate to the side, squeezed into the hole, and listened. The pipe was cramped and full of darkness. What if they spotted the opening? He would need to retreat no matter how hard it was to see. He felt his pocket for his Zippo and slipped it out. The pipe seemed to incline, like it descended downward the further he ventured.

"Albert. You in there?"

It was Elijah. Albert flicked his Zippo and turned and popped his head up.

"Here!"

Elijah screamed and fell backwards, knocking over a crate of wine. The bottles shattered inside the wooden box, and the dark liquid ran out from between the slats.

"I'll be John Brown!" he said, holding his hand to his chest and lying flat on his back. "You scared me to death!"

"I think I found it: the passage –under the suzie and drake just like Zephaniah said."

Elijah jumped up, stepped over, and leaned in toward Albert. Albert squatted in the pipe and flicked the Zippo again. The pipe glowed.

"Ain't you a regular Theseus, you hero. Now, hurry, we ain't got much time before them porters check here for me."

Elijah crawled into the pipe, and Albert lit his lantern. The light reached far into the passage that, just as Albert expected, took a deep turn downward. Albert turned around and sat, scooting down the steep pipe feet first.

He had done something: he had found a passage, and hopefully, it led to the treasure. He thought about Elijah's comment and wondered about this Theseus character. He had heard about him in school but must not have paid much attention that day. Was he big and strong like him? Did he save his family? Did he win riches? The exciting thoughts popped like kettle corn. Zephaniah's words had come alive; they had power. He was so enthralled that he never noticed that the smooth concrete of the sewer pipe had crumbled away to a rocky passage.

"Looks like we's in a cave."

They started a deep decent. To keep from falling, Albert lie on his stomach and slid down, his feet seeking a rock to brace himself. He descended after Elijah who struggled to hold the lantern at the same time.

"Elijah, who was Theseus?"

Elijah had gone quite a bit lower than Albert. He stopped and lifted the lantern.

"You almost at bottom, Albert; the cavern turns here to the right."

Albert inched his way down to the floor. The air smelled like dust. Sweat poured down Albert's face.

"Theseus was a hero who moseyed into a maze and saved some children."

"From what?"

"A bull man called a Minotaur."

Elijah turned and twisted down the cavern. Albert touched the cave walls. They were solid rock, so solid that all other noises died except for their own shuffling. Albert's earlier excitement evaporated as he remembered something Zephaniah had said– something about a giant. The old feeling of wanting to run welled up again. He crawled over a large rock and then squeezed through a hole.

"Elijah, do you remember what Zephaniah said about what was below the suzie and drake?"

Elijah stopped crawling and turned. "I think it was somethin' bout a giant and fight."

"What do you think it is?"

"Maybe a Minotaur," he said smiling, but then he kept going. Albert did not see the humor.

The tunnel meandered and turned, and they crawled for what seemed like hours. Elijah pushed forward, squeezing under large boulders and slipping through tight holes.

There was no stopping now; they just pushed forward, always pushing. That was Elijah's way since the beginning of the trip, and his persistence irritated like a speck in the eye.

Albert was exhausted, and although he moved, he fought to stay awake. His arms and legs ached. His knees bled. The cave felt like his kitchen on a summer day after Momma's baking. Stifling was the only way to describe it. To make matters worse, his mouth was caked with dust and he was thirsty. Just as quickly as he had been encouraged, he now wished for the journey to end, wondering if it might have been a mistake.

He was scared. Thoughts of dying flashed in his racing mind and the lone sounds of their scooting and crawling made him feel as if they raced to that end. They had been at it all day. Cotton filled his mouth. The water that had once surrounded them, only a crazy man would drink, but now even that was tempting.

"Blocked," Elijah said while pointing, and he stopped.

Albert looked through the dust-filled lantern light. A wall of rocks blocked the tunnel. Something stuck out of the pile, like some sort of tree limb. But as Albert looked closer, he shivered and felt sick. It was not a *tree limb*, but the limb of a human being.

"Oh, sweet Jesus."

Albert could not talk. Sweat poured down his head but he felt chilled. He scanned the cave ceiling above them.

"Let's check it out," Elijah said and moved closer. That was the last thing Albert wanted at the moment.

The rocks were like a pile of footballs. None were too big to move, but it would take a ton of work to get them out of the way, and worse than that, they would have to move the skeleton. But then what? There was always another challenge and maybe another cave-in.

Albert shook his head. He was sick of the obstacles. He was sick of the darkness. How much farther would they go if they did get through? Every time they had found a clue, it only led them to more struggles. He wanted to quit. Going back broke and poor was better than this.

"Lookie what I found here," Elijah moved a rock under the stretching hand, and he produced a crumpled, dusty twenty dollar bill.

"Let me see," Albert said and moved toward Elijah and took the bill. He had never touched twenty dollars before. The brittle piece of currency had the power to buy more food than his family ate in a week. "You know how many Hershey bars I could eat with this?"

"About a hundred," Elijah said and shifted more rocks, "but you gonna need some more to get you enough milk." He lifted another wad of twenties.

"This is it, Elijah! We found it!"

Elijah kept digging through the rocks. "Nah, this ain't it. No way it's all of it."

Albert's excitement settled some. "But it's enough, don't you think?"

"Enough for what? Shoo, it's only a couple a hundred or so."

"It's enough for us to go, to get outta here."

"Albert, you be's crazy. Kelly lost thousands, maybe tens of thousands. There ain't no way we be quittin now. We's just getting started." Elijah went back to moving rocks, sliding a larger one away, uncovering the smooth skull of the victim. Matted hair and some leathery skin still lingered in the dust.

Albert watched. His heart sank. They had money now, and they had their lives but for how long?

"Elijah, we are still living, and we got some money; let's go now before there's another cave-in."

"Albert, we is close. I can feel it. This here fella has some money. That means it come from somewhere down here I reckon. We'd be foolish to give up now."

"We're foolish to stay. I can't be a fool."

"What you say?"

"I can't go anymore. I quit."

"My ears can't believe they's hearin' this from your mouth. Quit? After all we been through?"

"It's too much, Elijah. Everything we've done has been hard and now the way is blocked. We got some money. When is it enough? We can't get through. I'm thirsty and..."

"You jus' scared."

"What?"

"You bein' a coward, I say. Albert, you've heard
the oracle, and if it wasn't for you, we probably
wouldn't be this far."

"I've had enough of your preaching and oracle
talk."

Albert turned and started scooting

"What 'bout our oath?"

"What?"

"Our oath. We promised to not run out on each
other. Remember that?"

Albert stopped and said, "But it's blocked.
Maybe the oracle was meant for someone else? We're
just kids."

"I think it's meant for you," Elijah said and had
that look in his eyes: the look that indicated he could
magically see into Albert. It was scary, like the
moment that Zephaniah stared into him as though he
had spotted something–something within his soul. He
did not want that look, did not want anyone to know
what lurked inside of him. He was sick of hearing
about his ability. He wanted to go home.

"I guess you run out on everybody when you scared."

That hit a nerve. He heard Pete crying for help. He saw the Sheriff fishing a body out of the river. Fury. Albert's head throbbed. He heard beating.

"Shut your mouth you dirty..."

"Nigger? Is that what you gonna call me? You think that's gonna hurt? Rather be that than a deserter!"

"SHUT UP!"

"That's what you did, isn't it? That's why you was all upset at the wash. You ran out on your family!"

"I SAID SHUT UP!"

Albert grabbed the first thing he touched which was a stone. It was instinct, uncontrollable. He screamed so loudly that his own ears hurt, and he hurled the rock. It whizzed over Elijah as he ducked. It would have killed him, but it missed. It deflected off a small rock in the middle of the rubble, and like billiard balls, several more crumbled. A small black void remained.

Elijah stared at the hole and pulled at the rocks around it. They crumbled away, opening up a tiny entrance to something dark and large on the other side. Albert breathed heavily and shook his head, hoping to erase the thoughts of what had just happened. Elijah turned, eyebrows still furrowed, but his anger melted away, and his familiar smile returned.

"I think we's through!"

Albert stared at the hole. He had never lost his temper before this. He could have killed his best friend, and it scared him to death. Tears gathered and dripped down his dusty cheeks, streaking mud along their path. He may have gotten them closer to the treasure, but at that moment, he did not feel like a hero.

Chapter Nine

Elijah and Albert tugged at the rocks with only silence passing between them. Albert's fingers were cut on the fractured stones. He yanked them back and winced from the pain.

Piling the loose rocks over the skeleton did little to hide its creepiness. Albert wanted nowhere near the creature, and an empty nervous feeling grew in his stomach each time he looked its way.

Another big rock separated and rolled out, making a hole large enough to see what was on the other side. Elijah ran the lantern through and looked.

"I thinks this is it! It's a big room. They is all sorts of stuff in here."

It was the time to feel excited, but Albert could barely look at Elijah because of the guilt he felt. He pulled another rock, and Elijah squeezed through to investigate. His opened hand poked back from the darkness.

"Lemme see the Zippo."

The darkness inside the hole felt like a hollow emptiness, and cold air poured from it into their smaller passage. When Albert passed the lantern, its glow was swallowed in blackness. But, in seconds the light grew and grew again, illuminating a cave room. His curiosity muzzled the murmurs of guilt and fear, and he squeezed through the hole. A lantern set next to Elijah's foot and another hung beside him on a spike. Elijah lit them too.

"Plenty of light," he said and smiled.

The room exploded with space. They had squeezed and stooped through one pipe after another–everything so close and tight–and now Albert stretched for the first time.

Long stalactites dripped from the ceiling like a cracked ice cream cone. Boulders and stalagmites congregated in places along the floor, but most of the cave was open, like the large lobby in The Peabody. All they needed was a piano.

The cave split into two levels. As Albert looked around the upper level, Elijah wandered down some natural steps along the right wall. He took the Zippo and lit a fourth lantern revealing stacks of mason jars and cans arranged on a rotten pallet. Cordwood lined the wall just feet from the cans. In between the cans and cordwood rested a large metal drum. It stood about four feet tall, a small pipe poked out from the top and twisted like a pig's tail downward into a coiling copper tube. The copper tube rounded and stretched toward the ground and poked through a smaller drum, coming out the other side.

"Well, I'll be John Brown. A moonshine still! Guess this was Kelly's production facility."

Albert swallowed hard and squeezed his eyes to fight back the tears as he remembered the screaming, the fighting, and the embarrassment in his home. Dad had drank from similar jars, and it was a good thing he was not here to fire the still and enjoy some brew. Kindness was a rare commodity when he drank from the jars.

Something splashed in the bottom of the cavern, and Elijah crept toward the sound. Thirsty was a mild description of the way they felt; it had been hours since their last drink. Nearing the noise, the lantern light reflected off a large expanse of water–a subterranean pond of some sort, and they rushed it. Elijah plunged his face and gulped. Albert stayed further from the edge and scooped the water with his hand. It was cold and remarkably fresh, but they would have drunk anything at that moment.

The pond stretched across most of the lower level and ended at a far rock wall that towered all the way to the cave ceiling. The wall must have stood nearly thirty feet to the top. Albert wondered if the water came from somewhere under the rock wall, like the artesian wells that Memphis was known to rest upon.

"You see that?" Elijah asked, lifting himself up and pointing to where he drank.

Albert had given up the scooping and had plunged his face into the water like Elijah. He raised his eyes from the oasis.

"Catfishes comin' to my light. I bet they is stuff up there to make a trotline and a fire. I don't know 'bout you, Albert, but I'm starved!"

Albert recoiled from the water's edge and wiped his hand on his overalls as if the water was acid. He hated catfish more than anything else in the world, and he wanted no part of trotlines. Memories flooded his mind of the night everything changed.

"I...I'm not much for the fishin' thing. I'll start looking for clues on the money," he said and started a retreat to the upper level.

Elijah looked a little shocked. "Ok, Albert, if you wanna go a lookin', I'll take care of the fishin'."

Obviously, that befuddled Elijah. Albert wanted to tell him it had nothing to do with their fight, but Elijah would only ask questions. Calling him that name was terrible, and throwing the rock at him was reprehensible, but he could not reveal his secret. With all that had already happened, Elijah would trust him no longer; the friendship would end.

Beginning at the cave opening, Albert lifted a lantern off a hook and scanned the area. Elijah rummaged through a junk pile beside the still.

"There's a ton of stuff here: matches, canned sardines—hope we's not reduced to eatin' them..." The pile clanked and clinked. "Hooks, rope, and twine.

Twine! Looks like 'Machine Gun' mighta done some fishin' down here himself."

Albert searched to the left, the opposite of the way they had already been and as far from the pond as possible. The stalagmites stretched from the floor like shark's teeth, and the cave wall disappeared into the dark. A rhythmic dripping provided background music and was interrupted only by Elijah's scavenger hunt.

Albert sighed. He was not sure what to even look for, and he wondered if the money they had found had anything to do with hidden treasure. He heard some rumbling from inside the cave entrance. He moved close and listened—nothing. Swallowing hard, he hoped it was not another cave-in.

Elijah returned to the water to catch dinner. He meandered along, spacing the lanterns where they would spread the most light. Then he stretched twine along the ground, which would serve as the mainline, and attached smaller lines called snoods.

Albert's job had always been attaching the snoods and the hooks. Pete claimed it was the secret to their success, that Albert's perfect spacing was the reason they caught so many fish. He always tied the hooks tightly, often pulling so hard the hook would slip and prick his hand.

Albert closed his eyes; another tear ran down his cheek.

He continued along the wall to get his mind off the past. The treasure, if there was one, had to be hidden down here somewhere. Since Zephaniah's oracle, they had found a moonshine still in an underground hideaway–a sure lair of a criminal. But where could the treasure be? It would make sense if Kelly had hidden the treasure here, but what if he had not? Or, even worse, what if it was already stolen? It was not a far-fetched idea, especially since they had found a skeleton with a wad of money.

A splash echoed, and Elijah bobbed and paddled in the dark water under glow of lantern light. He let out the line, having tied one end to a boulder. Once he was to the other side, he tied it off as the first, the line stretching across the middle of the pond. Then he grabbed a round rock the size of a loaf of bread and paddled to the middle where there was the most slack.

Albert gasped when he saw Elijah and took a step toward the pond, yelling, "Watch it, Elijah, don't let it tangle you."

"I think they is already one on the line! Fish is everywhere!"

Albert could not watch as Elijah tied the rock and dove under. Setting the weight rock was the most dangerous part, but it was necessary to keep the trotline submerged.

He could not watch and turned away, but then he spotted something along the cave wall, a depression or hole. If anything, it helped distract his worry. Perhaps it was a passage, a room, or a hide of some sort? He stooped and examined it. It was larger than most of the sewer pipes they had crawled through, but he still needed to be on hands and knees. He decided to chance it, but as he poked his head in and pushed the lantern through, he gasped.

A skeleton stared at him.

Albert jumped up, slamming his head. "DANG!" He scrambled backwards and rolled out of the hole onto his behind. His head throbbed and burned when he rubbed it. The skeleton was freaky, scarier looking than the one in the passage. It faced the hole like a doorman inviting him in, and that thought alone sent chills down his back.

He would not bother Elijah who had his hands full, singing as he yanked fish off as fast as he could bait the hooks. Besides, Albert had said this would be his job. He would inspect the scene himself. He took a deep breath and closed his eyes and entered, his hands and legs shaking as he crawled through the space

The small room smelled rotten, and the walls were covered in scratch marks, foul words, and rudimentary pictures—probably the creation of the host.

Tattered rags hung from the skeleton's brown bones. It was on its belly with its head turned. The hollow eye sockets glared, and the mouth, speckled with three teeth, gaped as if it was thrilled to have visitors. Beside its left hand set an opened mason jar, and by the right rested a dusty pistol. A long knife stood out from its back, jabbed between the ribs.

The mason jar caught Albert's attention, and he wanted to examine it, but it was funny how scary a skeleton could be. Albert knew it could not move, but there was still fear that that bony hand would clamp around his. Once, at Sunday school, the Sister had read in the Bible about an army of skeletons that rose up and lived. The hair on Albert's neck prickled, and he shivered as he drew closer.

The skeleton rested on some kind of mat, like a bed. Its death must have come during sleep, perhaps a payback after a drunken fight? Albert snatched the jar from the bony hand and scooted away. He dug inside, pulling out crammed wads of paper. He looked at a piece closely and dropped the jar which shattered on the rock floor.

"ELIJAH! I FOUND SOMETHING!"

***

"How much?" Albert asked, wiping his catfish greasy fingers on his pants. It was better than nothing, being so starved, but the more he imagined the catfish, its long whiskers and thin lips, the more his stomach turned. He wretched, turning quickly to barf behind some rocks just a few feet away. The acid

burned his nose and throat, and he smelled the
putridness.

"You okay, Albert?"

"Just not much for catfish."

"How can you live in Memphis and not like
catfish?"

"It's not the taste..." Albert stopped short of
giving any further information.

Elijah's face glowed in the fire. The hickory
wood cracked and popped, smelling sweet like a
barbeque pit, and Albert wished for some of the ribs
on Beale rather than the fish. The smoke rose,
gathered in a cloud, and disappeared. There was
somewhere for it to escape, possibly from the way the
still and equipment had been installed.

"Two hundred and twenty dollars," Elijah said
and piled the money into even stacks. "With what we
took from JR earlier, we be's at four hundred."

"JR?"

"Jolly Roger. I decided them skeletons needed
names. Makes 'em a little less spooky. Jolly Roger and
Old Bony. You like it?"

"I like the money."

It was the most either of them had ever seen. The pile of crinkled bills looked like crackly autumn leaves, but Albert saw more than money. There was a full dinner table: a round steamy roast, mashed potatoes and gravy, and laughing (how long had it been since they had laughed?) with dad kidding about mom's pickles. If there was more, there was a future. Dad would never slave for Butch Clines again, and maybe, just maybe, he would not need a drink.

"What do you think happened, I mean in that room with that knife and stuff?" Albert asked.

"Don't know. I bet Old Bony had the money all stuffed in the jar, and JR stuck him with the knife, making off with some of it. Then Old Bony shot at him as he ran, causing the cave-in."

"You think this is all of the treasure?"

"Hope not," Elijah yawned. "There was a ton of money the FBI never recovered, and if somebody stole it from this cave, that story would spread like wildfire. Nope, I thinks it is all still here, and our friends just so happened to find some of it. Their fightin' led to both buying the farm."

But where could it be? There were not many places left to look. Albert had almost traversed the entire cave and had only found "Bony's room." The pond covered most of the lower part.

But after a belly of fish (no matter how much he got sick) and a moment of sitting, he eyes grew heavy.

"I wonder about that mason jar..." Elijah yawned. "Found a rusty lid by the water."

"Who knows? My granddaddy used them to bury money in the back yard," Albert said, recalling a faint memory. "Not much, but enough for a rainy day."

"What you say?"

"He buried money in mason jars. He said the air tight jars would keep the bills dry."

Elijah raised up and said, "The water, Albert. It's in that there pond! The treasure is down there somewheres! That's why Bony had a jar, and the lid was by the shore!"

Elijah clapped, raised his hands in the air, and then folded them together in prayer, mumbling a thank you to Jesus. Albert, however, was not thankful at the moment. He shivered and his stomach twisted and fluttered, and he felt sick again. The water was the last place he wanted to look.

"We need to rest up 'cause we's got some swimmin' to do," Elijah said and he scooted around and got comfortable. Within minutes, he was snoring.

Albert was not sure he would be getting any rest. He had not swam since that terrible night, and he was not planning on it either. Thoughts racing, he wondered how he would get out of this mess. Pete flashed in his mind, neck deep in the river straining, pulling, screaming. Albert's shoulders slumped as if a pack was dropped on his back. He shook his head. The thought was too much. His heart felt like a lump of lead sinking in his chest.

He turned to Elijah who let out another blast. Albert lowered his head and lay down, left to bear the guilt alone—which was something he had been doing for two long years.

Chapter Ten

Murky water surrounded him, its cold cloudiness forced its way into his body, and his lungs burned from fighting it back. His heart slammed in his chest.

He must save him.

The fire in his lungs drove his desire to kick and break the surface, but he could not leave Elijah. His friend struggled, trotlines strangling and tugging at him. Albert yanked lines and threaded others to make sense of the mess, but the hooks punctured deep and pulled his cheeks and neck. He shouted and cursed, sounds muffled by the water ascending in a curtain of bubbles. Desperate, he pulled, pitting his brute strength against the string. He could not hold on, but he would not abandon Elijah.

A hand broke the surface and grabbed onto Albert's overalls, yanking him from the water. Albert screamed again and his fingers slipped from Elijah. He held his black hand and then his fingertips. Elijah mouthed something, bubbles floating around his frantic face. Then they lost their grip, and Elijah descended into darkness.

Albert screamed. The hand grabbed his overalls and yanked.

Dripping in sweat, Albert awoke from the dream, facing a man who gripped the bib of his overalls and pressed a knife against his cheek. The man reeked of sweat and sewage, and his breath smelled of whiskey. Albert nearly puked, and a chill ran down his spine from the good-for-nothing odor. The man looked familiar: the small face, round glasses, and the derby-capped, red hair. It was the crazed man from the store.

"Top of the mornin' to you," the man grinned. Muck smudged across his forehead and cheeks, and on his right hand—the one pressing the knife—was wrapped a bloodstained rag. A drop of sweat slid past his eye and pooled in his spectacles, one of which was cracked across the middle.

On the other side of the smoldering fire, Elijah lay on his side, ropes coiled around his arms, a dusty rag crammed in his mouth.

The skeletons, the cave-pond, the money: none of it was a dream. Albert woke into a nightmare.

The man clicked his tongue and shook his head. "Just like little boys who leave barn doors open, you two left the manhole cover off. Foolish. Just followed the commotion into the hotel like a bread-crumb trail." He looked up and around the cave, sizing up the area. "Looks like you were more useful than I thought. Aye, better than them other rats I dragged along," he said and grabbing some rope, he spun Albert around, yanking his arms behind him. "But they received the *justice* that was coming to them."

"What do you want?" Albert asked, voice quivering.

"What's coming to me: my share, my just reward."

Albert eyed the rusty blade that now rested on a rock. It was the knife that had been stuck in the skeleton's back. His heart sank to his stomach when he saw the old pistol stuck in the man's belt.

"Just let us go. You can have it, whatever you find. We won't tell anyone," Albert said.

"Oh, it's mine all right. It's been mine all along." He picked through the junk around the still. "George thought he could improve on my design, eh? Not gonna pay me for my recipes, eh? 'Machine Gun' was nothing but a fancy moniker for a petty cheat."

He screamed and accused his own filmy shadow, and then he turned to Albert and Elijah and laughed, a high-pitched chatter and then a howl.

"I will get my money, and you boys are going to be the ones to find it. You've done too good a job to quit now."

The man grabbed a piece of rope and cinched Albert's feet and forced him to the ground. Albert's shoulders cramped as his arms twisted.

"Finneous Schloper's my name. You've already met my good-for-nothing brother."

Albert did not understand

"He's where I got the knife," the man said and smiled. "Bastards thought they could take my designs and not pay me a dime; well, who's laughin' now?"

He looked over at the still. "WHO'S LAUGHIN' NOW?" he screamed. Pushing the glasses up his nose, he giggled and licked his lips, and then he pulled the cloth from Elijah's mouth.

"What's your name, Blackie?"

"I's more than a color!" Elijah said and squirmed to a sitting position. Finneous slapped him across the face, sending him backwards. Blood trickled from his nose.

"Your name, coon, or it'll be a fist."

"Elijah."

Finneous spun around.

"Albert, Albert McClune."

"Aye, a fellow countryman. What's your father's name?"

"Sean McClune."

He pushed his glasses up again. "Don't know a Sean McClune. Who came over?"

"My grandfather."

Finneous approached the still like an old friend and tinkered with the tubing.

"I'll have it workin' soon then start my own business, and I'll run things from now on," he said, and he dug around the pipe pieces and cans that piled behind the still. "Well, you boys have a great plan, I believe, so we are going to keep it going."

Albert felt sick again and his neck warmed.

"Can't have both of you dive'in in the water, though, no... one will have to stay for collateral. Big Boy, you are going to dive. Gotta have your muscle to bring up the loot. The coon will stay with me and show me how to catch these here...what you call catfish."

"I can't do it." Albert could hardly breathe at the thought of going into that deep, black water. Sweat poured from his forehead.

"Can't swim m'boy? You really an Irishman?"

"No, I can't swim," Albert said and stared downward, embarrassed. It was a lie, but there was no way he could enter water after that terrible night.

"That's a shame," the man mumbled and shook his head. "Hate to not have the fisherman with us."

And he walked over and picked up Elijah and threw him over his shoulder like a sack of potatoes. Elijah kicked and screamed against the ropes as Finneous lugged him down to the pond.

"STOP!" Albert shouted and squirmed in the tight ropes. They cut into his wrists as he writhed and turned. He did not know what to do. Elijah would drown.

The water splashed as Finneous tossed Elijah in with hands still tied.

"OH, GOD, NO!" Albert screamed and wailed. "NO, NO, NO, PLEASE!" He turned and twisted in panic. Elijah bobbed and coughed in the water. His head went under once, and he came up screaming, "ALBERT!" and then he went down.

Finneous moseyed up and cut the rope that bound Albert's feet and hands, and Albert sprinted toward the water. There was no time. Diving over the lanterns that glowed around the edge, he leaped into the cold pond. It had been two years since he had last swam, but he did not forget a stroke. It was as cold and dark as a moonless night.

He whirled around and reached out but could not find his friend. He neared hysterics but then felt a rope end. Yanking Elijah close, he kicked and went straight to the surface. As soon as he broke the water surface, Elijah coughed and gagged. Albert brought him to the side and Finneous pulled them out.

He stared at Albert with his cold ice-blue eyes. Albert would not return the look but just watched Elijah lying on his side like a caught fish, gasping for breath.

"You'll dive or Blackie dies," he stated as a simple matter of fact. "You'll have a moment till I return."

He swaggered to the smoldering leftovers of their fire and gathered some wood while humming a tune.

"Albert, what were you thinkin'? Can't swim?" Elijah whispered between coughs.

"I'm sorry; you wouldn't understand."

"Understand? What be's there to understand? You gotta dive or I'm dead!"

"I'm gonna try, Elijah, but I'm scared to death."

"You're scared? What you think 'bout me?"
Elijah hissed, then he took a deep breath, calming
himself. Finneous cursed at something in the pile and
shook his hand, bringing his finger to his mouth.

Elijah leaned in and whispered: "Tell me,
quick, what you scared of?"

It was too much. He could not know. Albert
slipped in the water and swam away toward the dark
corner, like he was heading to his own grave.

"I can't talk about it. I gotta dive." He could not
tell the truth. It was too horrible, and Elijah would not
trust him anymore.

Finneous revived the smoldering fire. The wet
wood cracked and popped, and the flames jumped
when he poured some moonshine on it. He filled two
more lanterns with fuel that was stored in an old tin
can.

"Albert! Wait!"

The lightless liquid swirled around him. He
deserved to die the same death as Digger that night.
Finneous paced down from the upper level holding
the lanterns and a roll of twine. With tears streaming

down his face, Albert took a deep breath and submerged.

The lantern light glowed above, hardly illuminating his way, and the cold pressed against his chest. His stomach hurt. Images of Pete rolled through his head, neck deep in the river screaming for help, straining and pulling with no result. Night fishing had turned nightmarish; the sheriff dragging a limp body from the current, tangled trotlines dangling from a dripping corpse. Memories he had buried deep inside haunted him while he aimlessly groped around slimy rocks and grime on the pond bottom—a fitting grave. He shivered and his lungs hurt from the held breath.

Let it in, let the water in.

It was an impossible task the man had put him to, ending most certainly in death, so why prolong the inevitable?

Then something swished by his face like one of the fans the rich women waved in church. It was a fin as big as his head! It slapped his cheek a second time, and his heart jumped as he raced to the surface.

Whooping and hollering met him as he broke the water.

"Did you see that thing?" shouted Finneous. "Get that line ready, boy!" Finneous pointed the pistol at Elijah who baited the trotline. "Catch me that fish!"

Albert gasped and splashed to the side. "I can't see anything down there, and that thing grazed me!"

"Then you've got a big problem," Finneous answered. "Look harder."

"But that thing is huge!"

Finneous grit his teeth, pushed his glasses up, and mumbled. He stepped over to Elijah who was starting toward the other side of the pond and grabbed him by the back of the neck. Slamming him to the ground, he jabbed the gun to the back of his head. Elijah grunted and moaned.

"Impossible?" asked Finneous.

"No, I'll do it, just stop hurting him!" Albert knew the words were empty, but he had no choice.

Finneous let go of Elijah, and Albert started toward the other side of the pond where the trotline stretched. Elijah stared desperately at Albert and mouthed "please."

He was trapped in a living hell. He breathed deep and submerged and considered where he would search first.

He returned to the surface for breath and watched Elijah work the trotlines, Finneous kicking and barking at his every move. The proud preacher-boy, silenced and defeated, worked his task with empty eyes.

Albert took a big breath and plunged under again, but this time he headed toward the rock wall. Going down feet first was too hard, so he turned his body and scraped his face against a crag. It hurt terribly, but he had to be tough. He kicked himself downward.

Except for the soft glow above him, it was pitch black, but worse than that was the silence. Only the occasional gurgle bubbled from ripples slapping against the rock. He was alone except for the monster that grazed him, and it had the opportunity in such dark water to suspend itself inches from his face.

His nose throbbed, but he continued to hold his breath. He thought about Pete again, how he screamed that night in the river, how he wailed the night the men took him away, blood pouring from his wrist. He thought again of just letting the water in, but he was too scared to try it, so he probed the rocks and grit.

The rocks he had head-butted were slimy, so he grasped them tight to keep his body from floating. His lungs started to burn and his head hurt. It was time for a breath, but he decided this time to keep his hands outstretched to avoid another bump. As he reached toward the rocks, he felt a void, like a hole in the wall. He twisted and pushed, breaking the lighted surface.

Elijah went into the water about the time Albert came up. He stretched another trotline from one side of the pond to the other. His right eye looked swollen—a sure sign that Finneous was beating him.

Albert was helpless. He had to search for the treasure, or it would be worse for Elijah, so he took another breath and submerged again. This time he had to hold it longer. He kicked and found bottom. Like a blind man groping for his cane, Albert felt for the void again. His searching was the thing that kept Elijah alive, so he searched hard.

It was amazing how darkness disoriented him. He would have bet money (if he had any) that he dove in the exact spot he had left, but all he felt was the same cold rocks. The burning returned to his chest and his head started to hurt again, but he wanted to push it–to go as long as he could without coming back up for air.

He examined the edifice, picturing how each rock felt when he touched them. Had the void been his imagination? The wall was mostly flat with a few sharp edges jutting from it, and then, as if obeying Albert's thoughts, it melted away again. He found the hole and he felt its edges.

The idea of entering would have never entered his mind before, but what had he to lose? He started in a few inches and then stopped. The giant fish flashed in his mind. Perhaps it was its lair? Catfish often lay their eggs in holes to protect them from other predators, and the last thing he wanted was to be trapped with a mad momma.

With his imagination wild and his lungs on fire, Albert kicked, broke the water, and gasped.

"Albert, you okay?"

Albert grabbed the wall, wheezing. He nodded, masking his earlier thoughts of Pete and the night. "I..." and he stopped short of revealing the hole. "I...haven't found anything."

"You still got plenty of places, Big Boy," Finneous interrupted. Elijah had climbed out of the water, and Finneous yanked his arms behind him and tied his hands.

"But I gotta have a break."

Reluctantly, Finneous pulled a pocket watch and popped the latch. "You'll have twenty minutes and not a second more." He snapped the watch closed, pushed Elijah down, and went off toward the still to tinker.

Albert shook from the weight of Pete's memory and the fear of the hole. He pushed himself up on the ledge as Elijah rested against a large rock. He looked bad–discouraged–and he had been the strong one the entire treasure hunt.

Elijah needed him, but Albert had felt so guilty of his past. All those memories stirred around and bubbled like a cauldron of soup. Finally, he confessed,

"I'm sorry I lied and almost drowned you. I'm also sorry about the rock I threw earlier."

Elijah closed his eyes for a few moments then said, "I forgive you, Albert, but you need to unload your burden. I know it's there. I been seein' it since we came near this godforsaken pond. What's in there?"

Albert did not want to say, but the words forced themselves out as if he were sick to his stomach. Tears flowed as he blurted out, "I killed someone once."

"What? What do you mean?"

He could barely speak. He had never told anyone, but the words just kept coming. "I didn't actually kill him, but I might as well have."

Elijah's face never changed, never dropped in shock. He stared intently at Albert, his right eye puffy and nearly shut. "What happened?"

Albert leaned close as the clangs and pings echoed off the cave walls from Finneous patching the old still.

"I used to go fishing with my brother Pete, running trotlines. I've spent lots of hours in the water mending and tying just like you, keeping the snoods a good even distance. You know, not too far apart, so

you could catch more fish on a single line. My brother
Pete knew all the best spots in the Wolf River; he just
had it in him to know where all the fish were, even
after storms. Huge catches every night we'd lug into
the kitchen. Dad's job wasn't so great but we ate good:
catfish po-boys, catfish soup, bar-b-qued catfish, you
name it; and Pete was the hero, he was *my* hero.

"You only got a few more minutes, you hear
me?" shouted Finneous. Elijah scowled in his
direction.

"Pete had a best friend," Albert said, pausing to
swallow hard. "Digger was what we called him. I think
his name was Douglas. Digger went fishing with us *a
lot,* and after a while, Pete took him instead of me."
Albert swallowed again. The tears gathered and
dripped down his cheeks.

Elijah stared at the floor, nodding as he
listened.

"Those nights I was left at home, I'd sneak out
and follow them into the woods to watch them run the
lines. Pete and Digger had all kinds of fun. I guess
they left me so they could talk about girls and stuff.
Night after night they brought fish home and my dad

beamed at Pete. But it was no longer Pete and me... it was Pete and Digger, and I hated him for it, hated him so much that I wished one night he would die."

Albert looked away for a second, silent, then continued.

"One night I watched them while they fished and something happened. Digger struggled in the water then went down; his foot must've tangled in the line, and the river, well, it just kept flowing. He popped up and went down again. Pete jumped in and tried to help, but the river was too strong. He lifted with all his might, trying to get Digger's head above the water. I should've jumped in, thrown a piece of rope, ran to the sheriff, but it was no use."

Albert confessed, "I can still hear his screams, but I did nothing, just froze. I never wanted Digger to die, but I was scared. I didn't want them to know I was spying. I didn't want to get in trouble for sneaking out. But, don't you get it? I could have done something and saved him."

He shook and wept.

"You been bearin' that burden of guilt all this time," Elijah said.

Albert rubbed his eyes and said, "Never have I fished again. Never wanted anything to do with the water. And Pete," he dropped his head and trembled, "Pete couldn't handle it. He blamed himself for not being able to save Digger. He went crazy from the nightmares and one day just snapped, even trying..." Albert could not say it. He remembered the blood splattering the kitchen floor, the Sheriff, the men in white.

Elijah was silent for a moment then he looked straight into Albert's eyes and said, "You is in need of forgiveness. Albert, this moment in here is a trial, a test. It is your penance."

"All right, you've had enough rest, m'boy, time to get back in," Finneous barked and stomped toward them.

"My what?" Albert whispered as he backed into the water.

"Penance: your chance to make it right with Pete and Digger. Your work in here is bigger than money, Albert."

"Get in that water before I distribute some of my own *justice*!" Finneous bellowed. His shadow loomed close in the glow of lantern light.

"Awake chief and find hope," whispered Elijah.

The words were familiar, but he could not place them, as if they were memories of long ago.

The oracle!

They were from the oracle, and so far, everything in it had happened. They were deep, and they were in a fight, and there was certainly a monster. It was almost eerie how the hypnotic words of Zephaniah lived before them.

He had to dive or Elijah would die, and diving would make him righteous, make him clean. No matter how hard it would be, diving was the only way to live.

Albert dove.

Penance. He had heard the word before, maybe in church. Elijah was a churchgoer and a preacher of sorts, but Albert's family rarely attended Mass. His dad just did not have much use for it, especially after Pete.

Yet he needed to be right with Digger and Pete, and the only way to do so was to dive and find the treasure and somehow set Elijah free—or die trying. He thought of the hole in the wall, and he kicked toward it and submerged.

His muscles throbbed and his head hurt. Exhausted, he forced himself to keep going and find the hole quickly. At the very thought of it, his stomach wretched. What if that giant was there? What if he got trapped? Or... what if it was an escape?

He felt against the wall and then found it. It was large, wide enough for two people to swim through. He thought of the fat, long lips of the catfish and those tentacally whiskers that twisted and turned. Penance was not easy, that was for sure, but the thought of forgiveness and freedom was enough to steel his nerves, so he pulled his body through.

Once inside the hole, he could not wait too long before he turned back, or he would never make it to oxygen. He would be trapped in the tunnel and drown in an underwater tomb. So he counted, estimating how much longer he could hold his breath. After about ten, the tunnel wall above him rose up, and his hand broke the surface. An air pocket! He raised his head, poking his nose and mouth above the water and breathed.

Albert stuck his hand right in front of his face, not able to trace its outline. He had never encountered such darkness, not even in the sewers. It was as if light had been destroyed. Hearing and touch would be his only guide, and with the confused echoes of his splashing, his ears were not too reliable. He figured, at the very least, he had found more than a small air pocket—probably not the lair of the giant and hopefully a way out.

He swam forward, groping in the dark, and then he stopped. If he were missing for too long, it would raise suspicions. Finneous would figure he had found some kind of breathing spot. He dove down and pulled himself through until he felt the opening and saw the glow. He raised and gulped air.

"Albert! You okay?"

Albert forced a cough and wheezed and pulled himself over to the side. It had to be a good piece of theater; it had to look like he had nearly drowned.

"There's no more time for rest, boy!" Finneous yelled as he pulled a fish off the line.

"Can't you see he's strugglin?" barked Elijah.

It must have been good acting.

Finneous jumped up and stomped over to the little prophet. With a coiled rope in hand, he beat his backside two, three, four times, and Elijah wailed.

Albert winced. He could not watch the rope slam Elijah's skin. He had to do something to appease the maniac. Diving down, he groped everywhere he could reach. He had to cover as much space as possible to eliminate areas and get closer to the treasure. He could not waste time with the air pocket, not for now. Elijah needed relief.

Pulling himself along the wall and past the hole, he plunged over and over. He released some air so he would not have to work as hard to stay on the bottom. This time he would count to see how long he could go before he needed to resurface.

He felt all along the wall until he found the bottom. Once he reached thirty, he felt a little burn; he had gone longer this time, his lungs grew stronger.

Groping and kicking, he meandered along, crawfish-like, feeling along the muddy riverbed.

He reached sixty. The burn was in full bloom. His head hurt but he kept after it. He needed to stretch out his time–improve his ability. He probed, but all he felt was rock and wall, then suddenly he felt another hole.

Eighty.

His head pounded and his lungs blazed, but he had to investigate. It was for Elijah. It was for Pete. He tried to think about them, not the pain. He focused his thoughts on the new find.

The hole was smaller and creepier than the one leading to the air pocket. He squeezed inside and it closed around him. Although he could not see, it just felt darker. The further he went, the larger the hole felt, but something loomed in front of him; he could feel it, feel its presence like someone staring. He reached and felt a long wormlike strand.

WHOOSH!

Albert slammed against the side of the hole. He blew the last of his breath and swallowed water. A slick body and fan-like fin slapped him, cutting his face and chest. He scrambled and guarded his eyes, but the fish smacked and barged past him as quick as he had felt the whiskers. Dazed and panicky, Albert felt around for the opening. There was something cold and round in the mud, and he snatched it as he exited.

He was out of time and near drowning. Paddling to the surface, he hit the air, coughing and gagging. It took every ounce of his energy to pull to the side.

"You see that?" Finneous yelled. "Never seen a fish that big!"

"Did it fin you?" Elijah asked. His eyes were red and a trail of blood ran from his nose around his mouth.

Albert nodded and retched and belched pond water. Finneous jogged over and yanked him up.

"Did you find anything?"

Albert pushed up on his belly and rolled, revealing a muddy mason jar, its brass ring corroded and slimy. Finneous snatched it and strained to twist the lid, so he took it and cracked it against a rock. The glass shattered, and a tight wad of green landed and expanded as if taking a breath.

Albert and Elijah stared. A wad of crinkled one hundred dollar bills lay crumbled in the glow of lantern light.

"I FOUND IT! I ACTUALLY FOUND IT!" Finneous hollered and danced a little jig. "After ten years, he's paying up now, oh, with interest."

"You finally happy now?" Elijah barked. He could not help mouthing-off to Finneous. Elijah was independent and strong, and he refused to be anyone's slave.

Finneous looked up at Elijah and took one step and backhanded him. Albert stood, his fists balled, and Finneous drew the pistol and cocked the hammer.

"He's cheated me for years, and you're not about to take it back!" He pulled the pocket watch from his dirty trousers. "You've got ten minutes, then back in the water to get the rest."

Finneous walked away counting the cash and cackling, mumbling about his revenge on Kelly. He put it in his pocket and went back to checking the trotlines, cracking another can of sardines to attract the monster fish.

"Found its hole, that's for sure." Albert touched his cheek. The long, raised whelp burned at the touch.

"Biggest catfish I seen, Albert, as big as you!"

"It lives with the money."

"Is there more?"

"Not sure, but we'll learn soon enough."

Chapter Eleven

It took nine seconds to swim to the treasure hole from where he and Elijah rested. Everything was now a number, a time, in relation to his ability to hold a breath. He had worked up his stamina to over a hundred, so he knew he could do plenty of out of sight activity. Once before the hole, he probed carefully, feeling for the catfish.

Nothing.

Maybe his earlier invasion was enough to scare the monster away? Once inside, the hole opened up to a big underwater room. He swept his hands along the bottom. Round tops of mason jars studded the floor of the hole like a plowed potato field. There were so many that Albert forgot about his breath count and figured he would start again at twenty.

He had an idea. He grabbed four jars, putting two in his big pockets and holding the other two like a football, then he swam in the direction of the big wall. Ten more seconds is all it took to reach it.

Finding the opening, he paddled through until he reached the air pocket. He neared sixty, so he did not have much time. Feeling around, he found the rocky ledge. It was just wide enough to hold two rows of jars. Once he placed the jars on the ledge, he dove again. He reached the treasure hole quickly and grabbed two more jars and surfaced, gasping. He had been under water for a little more than one hundred seconds, long enough for it to seem like a difficult dive.

Elijah squatted near the "fishing" ledge. He fiddled with the trotlines while Finneous towered over him with the gun. Albert paddled to other the side, careful to not swim too close to the lines, and he set the jars on the rocks. The water dripped from the muddy glass and pooled on the stone.

"Keep working that line!" Finneous snapped as he trotted around the pond. He seemed more like a scavenging hyena than a man.

"How many are there?" he asked. It was time for Albert's act.

"I don't know. They're scattered and the hole's deep. I felt around and found one every so often."

Albert forced himself to look Finneous straight in the eye, and for once, lying came easily. He had never been able to do it with his dad, but this *mis*information could be their only hope.

"There's more. I know there's more. Kelly wouldn't have gone to the trouble for only a few thousand, keep looking."

"Maybe those two skeletons took more than we think?"

"Impossible."

"I need a break."

"You can have one when you find more."

"I'm exhausted."

"Fine, you take a break," the man pulled the knife from his belt "and I take a finger." He walked around the pond to Elijah and grabbed his curly hair, yanking him toward the ledge. He dragged him away from the lines and pressed his hand against a rock.

Elijah wailed as he pressed the blade against his fingers.

Albert was almost sick with horror. "PLEASE!" He screamed. "I'm going, I promise!"

Finneous looked up and grinned, savoring his little two-ring circus. Elijah's hand bled but his fingers were still attached.

"You can rest and eat in a couple of hours. You'll work until then."

Elijah trudged back to the area where the trotline had been set. He had the worst end of the deal serving as Finneous' punching bag. The captor poured all of his frustrations onto him: if a fish fell off the line or the fire died down, it was somehow Elijah's fault.

Elijah was a pariah and his head hung. Tears ran down his face, pouring out from his darkening eyes. The spark that they had had, so full of hope, had all but faded.

That was Pete's same look after the fateful night. He had wept and struggled to keep Digger's head up, but when he breathed his last, Pete went dark.

This was Albert's one chance, his penance, and penance involved pain. Despite the ache in his arms and legs, he was committed; Elijah would not die like Digger, and Albert would not abandon him.

There must be a way of escape. The air pocket and his newfound shelf for the jars had to be the key. Finneous was starting to panic about the money, and Albert knew better than anyone that panic led to stupid mistakes. Finneous's greed would blind him to important details, and Albert welcomed the advantage.

The catfish looked nothing like cave fish which were all white and blind; it was grey and brown, just like he had caught (in smaller versions) for years. They were from the river, but somehow they entered the cave pool.

The Goliath-fish was also nowhere to be found, as though he had just disappeared; and a fish that big could hardly go unnoticed in an area so small, not with all their activity. If a fish that big had found a way in, there must be a way out.

It was time to explore the cave pocket, to see if there were any clues, and at the same time, he had to appear busy treasure hunting.

He dove and grabbed more mason jars. Still fearing the fish's return, he rushed out of the lair. Elijah had said that the catfish was as big as him, a giant. The old blacks that fished on the riverbanks would talk about "cats" half as big as a man. Some were crazy enough to noodle: plunging their hand into the catfish lairs, wiggling their finger like a worm until SNAP. They would yank the fish out of the water, its mouth clamped on their fist.

But no single man would snatch this fish from its hole. It was a monstrosity and was quick to sting, which Albert had already felt from its ice-pick fins. The last thing he wanted was another attack.

He paddled to the air pocket to catch his breath and set the jars on the ledge. From what he had witnessed busting out of the first jar, there had to be a ton of money. He went down again and brought another two jars to Finneous who giggled and danced when he broke them open.

If the maniac knew how many jars were really down in the hole, he would slit both of their throats.

Nevertheless, with Finneous giddy over greenbacks, Elijah had less trouble. So it was time to do some exploration of the air pocket.

Albert dove into the hole and raised his hand to find the ledge. He touched the jars to make sure they were safe. Then he continued along the wall. The wet stone smelled musty and metallic. Every drip and splash echoed. Hopefully, he could determine how far it stretched, but he had to keep in mind his count. He moved along for another few seconds until his fingers bumped something: a jar, and it plopped into the water. He had circled the room!

The air pocket was a dead end, at least above the water, but what about below? It had barely taken him half a minute to circle the hole, so he counted as soon as he went under. Pulling his way along the wall, he felt some slimy branches and a small opening. He stuck his hands through it, imagining its width. It was barely as wide as his shoulders, if that. Elijah would easily make it, but there was a chance Albert would be hung up. And who knew if the hole even led outside or how far it went before they could get to air?

He had been gone long enough. Finneous would suspect something soon. He surfaced, caught another breath, and went back to the cavern. Then he continued his work, gliding over from the treasure hole to the air pocket to the treasure hole to the surface. All along, he considered the small hole and the possibility of escape.

The smell of roasted catfish wafted in the air, and even Albert's stomach screamed for filling. He swam to the side where Elijah leaned against a rock, completely exhausted, his hands bound. Albert shivered from hours in the water, his palms all wrinkled and white, and his legs felt as heavy as tree trunks.

Finneous stepped down from the upper part of the cave carrying a dented tin plate. Two catfish sizzled, charred on one side and nearly raw on the other.

"Better eat up. You'll be having to clear out a cave-in pretty soon... that is, once I get all my money and catch that bastard," he said and pointed. "If you live through that, I might let you go." He untied Elijah and walked back to the still and the fire.

"I doubt that," Elijah mumbled. "The one thing we ain't gonna do is live."

Albert grabbed a fish and ate, not caring if it was half cooked. He wished he could chomp on bones and all, anything to fill his emptiness. Finneous settled up top to tinker with the copper tubing. He mumbled to himself, demanding his rights and bragging of his accomplishments.

"I think I've found a way out," Albert whispered to Elijah.

"Where?"

"Well, it's a long shot, but it may be our only chance. There's an underwater tunnel in that rock wall. I think it goes to the river. I've hid a ton of money in there."

"I thought you had a hard time findin' the money?"

"I lied. It's everywhere. I'm timing my dives to make it seem like I'm struggling to find jars."

Elijah smiled. "I been tryin' to teach that idiot how to fish. He's obsessed with catchin' that Goliath–

had me doublin' twine so it wouldn't break it this time–even had me tie on pots to alarm him."

"Did it work?"

"Fish ain't come. Smartened up."

Albert sat silent for a minute and then smiled. "What?"

"We just gotta find a way to get you out of the ropes."

"I don't figure how that's gonna happen. He only unties me when he's needin' help."

Albert thought again and said, "So as long as I'm around, you aren't free. Guess I need to drown," he smiled.

"What? Don't be talkin' like that."

"Look, I'll be fine, but you gotta play it up. Soon, you'll be diving cause he's gonna need help."

"You want me to find the hole and follow?"

"No, just dive like he says. Then I am going to distribute some of my own *justice.*"

Finneous stepped down toward the water and examined his fishing lines. He toted a burlap bag to collect the ones he pulled off the hooks. Albert prayed the giant catfish would not return. Finneous looked at him and said, "All right, Blackie, fishes are on the line. Time to get back to work, Albert."

Albert's heart raced. He decided to move a few more jars before he enacted his plan. He slipped into the water and winked at Elijah. Courage and timing would be everything.

He dove again and grabbed four more jars from the hole and shot over toward the tunnel. He had swum the circuit enough times that he barely felt for direction. He had learned how to get around in the darkness just like the old fish. He popped his head up in the secret cavern and inhaled. He set the jars on the ledge with the others and returned to the cavern. Finneous would get no more.

It was time for his best acting. He popped up and swam to the side breathing hard, coughing. "That's it, I can't find anymore."

"What?" Finneous marched over.

"I've gone deep, deep as I can in the hole."

"Is the hole deeper?"

"Yes."

"Then go deeper. There must be more."

Albert had him hooked and he kept up his act. Unfortunately, it would probably involve pain to Elijah. "I can't. I can't hold my breath that long."

Finneous stomped over to the edge that Elijah worked and grabbed him by his hair and slapped his face repeatedly.

"I'll try! I promise! Just don't hit him again!"

Albert grit his teeth, scorning Finneous and despising his own charade of inability. It hurt Elijah, but he had to continue, and with a little luck, Finneous would pay for his cruelty.

The Irishman walked over to his lines, and Albert dove, but this time he would not return—not until he knew Elijah was in the water.

Chapter Twelve

Keeping time in the darkness was next to impossible as Albert reviewed each element of his plan. Elijah had to be swimming, searching for treasure, that was key. Timing was everything, and any amount of impatience could be disastrous. He had to keep his mind occupied.

Albert touched the ledge, feeling for the jars that he had found. The rocks were cold and slick from the constant wetness. He could try the Zippo and see if it still worked. Old men at the barbershop would often brag about what their lighters had been through and which brand was the best. Digging around in his chest pocket, he pulled it out, flicked it open, and shook the water out of the wheel and flint. It was probably too wet, but it was worth a shot. He ripped the wheel, nothing. Spinning it again and again, he was about to give up, and a sizzling spark shot out in the dark. Oily odors of burning lighter fluid filled the air pocket. Albert flicked it one more time and the flame popped and held.

He set it on the ledge with the jars. The glow revealed the passage, and just as Albert thought, it was barely bigger than a camping tent. If he pulled himself high enough in the water, he could scrape the dusty ceiling, and it would only take two strokes to get to the back wall. Except for the hole he had found earlier, it seemed this was only a room—a dead end.

He counted the jars on the ledge, careful not to knock one in the water, "13...14... 15..."

Fifteen jars could add up to thousands of dollars, especially if they were as packed as the others. Carrying that many jars underwater would be impossible. He would have to find a sack of some kind.

Getting out: that was the real problem. There were no guarantees that the hole below was the way out. He reached for the Zippo on the ledge and bumped it over. It toppled and slid off into water and the cave went black.

"Dang it!"

He held his breath and dove, groping along the bottom, and he felt a fin graze his face. He rushed to the surface. The catfish was there. His heart raced. Had a catfish ever killed a person? But then, just as quickly, he thought about the hole. With catfish meandering in this pocket, it was probably the way to the river.

He guided himself again to its location. Just a few feet under the surface rested the opening. Fresh water seemed to push through the hole, but he was not sure. It could lead to the river, and he could be just feet from freedom, but he would never know unless he chanced it.

He felt the hole and pulled himself in only to find that his shoulders scraped the sides. He saw no signs of light, only the blackness that was of an endless tunnel.

Doubt set in. The cold dark grave closed around him. He retreated and surfaced. There was no testing it, they would only know by taking the risk.

He fought back the fear. Surely it was the way. How else could all these catfish get in here? They were channel cats and blues, so they had to be from the river, and this had to be an inlet, but how far would they have to swim to get out of it?

He wished Elijah were there. If anything, he would have an old story, some tale of Thesis or Thebets or whoever it was that acted like a hero. His tidbits may have been annoying in the Shanties, but they helped him over the rough spots.

He had waited long enough. It was time—time for the Goliath catfish.

Gliding back to the ledge, his heart thumped. Death was certain if the plan did not work and guaranteed if he did not try. He sucked in a deep breath and disappeared into the darkness.

Reaching the trotlines quickly was pivotal, but he had to be careful of the snoods. If he hooked himself in the long lines, tangling would soon follow, then the entire trotline could wrap him up, and he would suffer the same fate as Digger. He cleared the tunnel and kicked, his arms outstretched like sonar. The water seemed bright compared to the dark passage, and he was able to make out the bank and a skinny silhouette that paddled above him. Elijah was in the water!

Kicking his tired legs, he neared the trotlines. The meat-baited hooks hung quietly, like an undersea minefield. Finding just the right snood would be the trick, it needed to be near the ledge but still close enough to the other snoods that hung from the main line.

A fire sparked in his lungs. He blew a few bubbles.

Probing along the bottom, he brushed against a line. He steadied himself and slowly ran his hand along it, counting the snoods. Elijah had tied them about a foot apart. Several hooks were bare and others revealed sharp points, the fingerlings having nibbled away the sardines. He slid his hand gently down the main line to the bottom of the lake where Elijah had weighted it with a coffee can sized rock.

His lungs burned now. He had to work quickly or all would be lost on his need for air. Untying the weight rock was easy, and the line relaxed and swirled in the water like a snake. Avoiding it was the hard part for slack was deadly, especially in dark water where he could not see its swirls and turns. In seconds the free-floating line could catch his clothes and it would be over. He swam up the line and found the ledge and yanked the nearest snood.

In the lantern light above, the float jumped and bobbed like an injured fish. Albert heard his heartbeat, felt the pulsating in his head. He needed air, but there was no time to swim back to the tunnel. This was it. He was committed. He pulled hard on the line again and felt a tug back. Then he blew some bubbles and watched.

Looming overhead, a shadow darkened the glow, and a hand broke the surface. Albert grabbed the line and pulled again and the hand yanked in response. He tugged and it tugged in return. Then he coiled on the bottom, squatting low like a spring, and pulled as hard as he could. As soon as he felt the tug, he sprung, pulling the line downward as he shot upwards through the swirls.

Water exploded from his surface break. Finneous stumbled, eyes wide in shock. Albert gasped and grabbed and yanked the moonshiner into the pond. He was rabid.

Finneous swung blindly, panicking, his fists splashing, hitting anything he could. But with head down in the water, Albert worked his hands, wrapping the line like a hungry spider, twisting his web around Finneous's feet, neck, and arms. Finneous growled and flailed and then became still. Albert pushed off of him with his feet, a hook catching, tearing his heel.

"YOU LITTLE BAST...!" Finneous bubbled and bobbed. A hook ripped into his cheek, and twine strangled his neck and arms like a Water Moccasin. The float bounced on his head as he fought to keep above water. The more he struggled the worse he tangled.

Elijah stared, mouth gaped.

"Get the fish sack!" Albert yelled. "There's not much time!"

Finneous cursed and fought toward the side, submerging twice. Panic plastered his face.

Elijah jumped out and grabbed Finneous' catfish bag; the knife rolled out and plopped in the water.

"For sure can't get out up top, the cave-in is big."

"Get in the water and follow me!" Albert yelled, and Elijah jumped in.

"JUSTICE!..." Finneous bubbled and went down again.

Albert swam to the wall and then submerged. Elijah had jumped in behind him and grabbed his pants leg. Albert led his partner through, and the two surfaced in the dark safety of the air pocket.

"We beat 'em Albert! We's safe. Now what do we do?"

"You have the burlap?"

"Right here."

Water splashed from the bag. Albert felt for Elijah's hand and moved the bag closer to the ledge.

"I put fifteen jars on the ledge. Well, sixteen, but I dropped one. Now I'm going to empty them into the bag. Keep it still so I know I'm dumping the money in the bag and not the water. Then we gotta chance a way out."

"You think this here tunnel goes all that way?"

"It goes only a few feet," Albert said, twisting lids and dumping the cash and dropping the empty jars in the water, "then we gotta dive. There's an opening smaller than what we just came through that leads to the river."

"How so?"

"The catfish. They..."

"Don't look all white like somtin' dwellin' in caves," Elijah finished the thought. "Not bad thinkin', Prince."

"I'm not..."

"Wit all that money? Shoo! We's both princes!"

The boys laughed, and Albert emptied the final mason jar in the bag. Elijah closed it tightly in his fist.

"Wait here."

Albert dove and moved along the wall. It was silent under the water with the occasional sounds of the bubbles he blew. The sense of touch was all that mattered at the moment. His fingertips became eyes, and he pictured every rock and how far he had moved. The smooth indention gave way to the hole; the slimy branches poked Albert's shoulder. He felt the opening from top to bottom and then the sides. It was small, possibly too small for him to fit. Something slick brushed his hand. It slapped and darted away–a catfish passed through the hole. Albert turned and surfaced.

"I found it," he said, "but there's a problem."

"What?"

"You'll fit for sure, but it may be too small for me."

"Any other ways?"

"Don't think so. I felt a catfish swim through. I think it's our only chance."

"The catfish is a good sign, the hole ain't. What you wanna do?"

"I think we have no choice but to chance it and soon. I don't know if Finneous is dead or not."

"I be ready, Albert. What's yo plan?"

"You need to practice holding your breath. I don't know how far we'll have to swim. In fact, we may not make it, but we gotta try. When I first dove, I couldn't hold my breath very long before it burned. I've kept doing it and was able to get to almost two minutes."

Elijah sucked in a deep one and held.

Albert counted. He reached thirty before Elijah exhaled.

"You gotta practice some more. I don't know how long this cavern is. Go under. It'll force you to hold it longer."

Elijah bobbed down then up, staying under longer each time, breaking the surface and gasping in the dark. Albert counted each time; he had worked up to nearly a minute.

"Now, I'll guide you to the hole. You'll go through first with the bag so you can pull me though if I get stuck."

"Got it. Then what?"

"We pray the cavern isn't too long."

"You more like Theseus than you think."

Chapter Thirteen

The darkness was dense, the water cold. Albert felt for the opening and tugged Elijah's shirt, leading him to the passage. Elijah squeezed through. Albert felt the edges of the opening. The broken branches poked through like spears. He sucked in his gut and entered, working one shoulder through, then the other, but he got stuck at the waist. A sharp end poked through his pocket. Elijah tugged on his arm.

Fifteen seconds ticked away, and they needed every one of them, but no amount of yanking could loosen the soaked denim. Time ticked away, and though Albert knew how long he could hold his breath, but he was not sure about Elijah. He pushed with his feet, digging and shredding his toes on the rock floor.

Elijah pulled again–still no movement. Albert felt desperate. He had to get through or they would die in the hole.

Elijah braced his feet and pulled as Albert pushed. His overalls tore a little and he felt the give. That was all he needed, and he snapped off his straps. Elijah pulled again and Albert, in his underwear, slipped right through the dark hole.

But there was no time.

The struggle had lasted for almost a minute, an eternity when holding a breath. Elijah had to be hurting; Albert's lungs boiled. Water tried to force its way in him again, proving to be a relentless foe. He kicked and felt along the top of the tunnel and pulled himself forward with one hand while dragging Elijah with the other. Swimming forward was now their only hope.

He reached one hundred and still no air. Every inch ahead was a prayer for breath. Only seconds left and it would be over. Elijah slowed his kicking. He was giving in.

Albert yanked him close and continued pulling through.

How much farther?

His cramping arms seized; his body starved for oxygen.

Keep kicking.

Pulsating filled his ears. He saw spots in the darkness and he stopped counting, only remembering one hundred and thirty two.

Was this penance: his life for Digger's?

Time was up, time to die. He reached to grab one last rock and felt the cool emptiness of air.

Air.

It was there ready to be consumed. He surfaced and gasped and lifted Elijah who had already sucked in water. He gagged. They heaved and coughed. Spit flew from Albert's mouth. Elijah threw up.

Tears streamed down Albert's cheeks, and in between wheezes, he laughed.

"You still got the bag?"

Elijah nodded.

Albert saw the gesture. He had moved in darkness for so long that seeing his friend was a shock. Light entered from somewhere.

Moonlight lit the tunnel, not much, but enough to see Elijah. Through an opening behind them, the round ball bounced along waves–the Mississippi on a bright night. Albert waded toward the opening. Reeds rustled on each side and waved in the dark currents. Looking out of the grassy hole, he watched the water pass one way and the lonely tugboat lights fighting up the other direction. The river smelled of rotten fish and rancid mud, and the tugboat motor hummed along the swirling currents. A deckhand rang a bell, and the horns blew long and low, like a pipe organ in a church. The odors and sounds were more than welcome.

"What do you want to do?" Albert asked.

Elijah, still coughing, answered, "Let's swim out, catch a current to the bank and watch."

"Sounds good to me. I love the tugboats, and I gotta dry out."

Albert pushed out into the open. Stars dotted the black sky above; he had missed the sky, the open expanse. The water was cool, the current forceful, pushing him along like a small log.

"You know, Elijah, I thought about running away on one of those tugboats."

An empty silence followed.

"Elijah?..." Albert looked all around. "ELIJAH!"

He swam back against the current to the hole, peering all around the bank to see if Elijah had scampered up a side. He had just touched bottom when he heard a splash. A tall silhouette rose above him and yanked his hair.

"DROWN ME? TAKE MY MONEY?"

Hooks still dangled from Finneous' bloodied, distorted face. He slammed Albert's head into the water. Albert flailed. Finneous dunked him again.

"YOU THOUGHT YOU WERE SO SMART, LIKE KELLY?" he rasped and wheezed.

Down again. The river rushed into his nose and mouth. He pushed up but it was no use; Finneous was too strong, too angry. Albert was drowning. He had to cough, had to get air. The more he struggled the harder Finneous pushed on his head. He hit and slapped but it was no use.

Up again. Albert coughed and gagged.

"See this you little bastard," he said, lifting the money-filled bag, water pouring then dripping from it. "It's mine! Nobody will thieve me again, *justice* I tell you, *justice*!" And he plunged Albert down for the final time.

It was a baptism unto death. Albert was spent. The flailing stopped and he relaxed. Water slithered in, choked his throat, and all went dark.

***

Gasp.

His lungs longed to explode. They were full. He forced air in with all his might.

Coughing, wheezing, gagging, spitting.

"Lean dat boy over."

He felt a hand rolling him. He rocked, a metallic thump, sloshing, bubbling. There was water before his eyes, but he was not in it.

A boat.

He leaned over the side and threw up river water. He hacked some more and felt the boat bump and scrape along the sand.

"Les lift him up and on da bank." The voice was not Elijah, but familiar.

Hands grasped under his arms, dragging him out of the boat and onto rocks and then soft grass. His throat and nose burned from his stomach juices.

"I'll git some wood for a fire."

It sounded like Elijah, but in the moonlight, it was hard to focus. A shadow loomed over him. Long tube-like hair dangled around his face. The specter touched his cheek and his chest, humming, singing strange sounds, unknown words. Albert closed his eyes.

He woke again to the sound of pops and sizzles and smoky wood smells. A fire danced in a ring of river rock. His chest burned from the heat, but his backside was chilled. Wearing nothing but dirty damp underwear, he drew his knees to his chest to cover up.

He had no idea where he was, along the river somewhere. His first thought was that he had died, but this place was closer to home than heaven. The fire cracked around the driftwood throwing light on a familiar face, dark and bearded with long strands of hair that hung on each side of his face like curtains.

Zephaniah.

He squatted and gripped a long stick, the muscles rippling on his arms. He was stronger looking than Albert remembered. He turned three skewered fish over the fire, their fat sizzled, and their grey skin blackened and shriveled in the heat.

"Elijah, your white boy is up."

Elijah bound from behind Zephaniah and walked over to Albert.

"You okay, Albert? How you be feelin?"

His head throbbed and his muscles hurt, but it was better than dead.

"I'm all right. What happened?"

"Bout the time you waded out in the river, Finneous slipped up behind me, knocked me on the head. I almost drowned. He had somehow followed us, crazed from your trick."

"The money? Is it lost?"

"I gots it, don't you worry. Pure luck on findin' it though. It had floated into some brush after Zephaniah got him. Finneous had almost killed you."

"Zephaniah got him?"

The Haitian smiled. It was the first time Albert felt he meant it.

"I was on a good fishin' hole, and yo' little ruckus, Whitey, ruined my catch."

He pulled the fish out of the fire and inspected the meat. He handed one to Elijah and stretched the stick over to Albert. The smoky flesh made his stomach growl. Albert grabbed the fish and tossed it between his hands. He peeled the blackened skin and flaked off a piece. Rolling the sweet white flesh around in his mouth, he closed his eyes. "Thank you."

"Whitey, you also owe me a knife. Lost it in that Irish pig," he said and winked. "Now listen to me. It'll be light soon, then you boys gotta leave. He'll wash up down river if he hadn't already. Then da police will be a lookin'. Two half-dressed boys carrying a sack of cash is gonna make them wonder."

"Take some money, please... for my life."

"It's yo money. The oracle was bona fide for you. If I take it, it'll be bad voodoo for me, and dats the last thing I need. Now, stay along the river, and take cover when you see folks." Zephaniah stood and dusted off his dirty trousers. "I'm headin' back. Eat da rest of them fish."

Although Zephaniah scared him to death, Albert was sorry to see him go. "Thank you... for helping me."

Zephaniah smiled and waltzed down the bank, grabbing the bow of the canoe and shoving it out into the water. He dug in with his paddle and disappeared in the dark. His eerie songs faded in the distance.

Elijah shook his head. "I know he says we gotta lay low tomorrow, but somehow we gotta find you some clothes."

Albert snapped up from his fish. "How? Zephaniah said we'd look too suspicious."

"I don't know, yet, but they ain't no way I'm travelin' with a white boy in underwear. That's just plain weird."

They laughed and talked and drifted to sleep; the most peaceful sleep Albert had had in days.

Chapter Fourteen

"Albert, wake up!"

Albert rolled over in the wet grass and shivered. Thankfully, the night was warm and his sleep was deep. His skull throbbed, and he could hardly move his arms and legs from the stiffness. A slight breeze swept across the surface of the rolling river. Just feet from the bank, a feeding gar splashed, slapping the swirling water.

The police. The thought rushed in on him, making his heart race. It would only be a matter of time until the body was found. They had to get moving. He forced his legs under him, rolled onto his knees, then stood up on wobbly-tired feet. He crossed his arms to cover his grass-plastered, bare skin, but it was futile—arms were not useful in covering his cold nakedness.

A low whistle sounded. It was a tugboat churning upriver, pushing a barge of timber. Waves rolled out from behind it and began their rhythmic slosh against the shore, releasing smells of muck and rotten fish. Elijah began stacking some shoreline rocks, their clacking echoing on the misty morning bluffs.

"Where are we going?"

"To get you some clothes. I got me an idea last night, but we gotta hide the money in these here river rocks in what old trappers used to call a cache." He stuffed the burlap in the hole and covered it with a jagged brown stone. He marked it with a piece of long rotting driftwood.

"Let's just walk on home and hide when we need to," Albert said.

"That's just it: we won't make it back. They is lots of people that come around here, and there is few places to hide. They'll take one look at us and know we's been in a scrape with somebody."

"What are we going to do?"

"We're jumpin' out of the pan and right into the fire. Go right into the middle of folks, and you'll be missed. It's gonna be a little embarassin', but it'll make us less suspicious."

Elijah trudged up the bluff toward the looming buildings.

"We're going to the streets? Are you crazy?"

"We's could go back in the sewers. No map. Chance being washed into who knows where?"

"No... I've had enough of sewers for a while. Just remember: you're not the one in your underwear." Albert reached down and found an old newspaper and wrapped it around his shoulders like a cape. It waved in the morning breeze.

"You ain't gonna be for long. Trust Elijah."

They crossed the railroad tracks and plodded up a steep street. Cars rambled by, the drivers staring, and Albert averted his eyes with embarrassment. His cheeks burned. He could not take much more.

"How are we going to lay low if we're walking toward all the people?"

A police car rounded the corner and sped down the bluff, siren howling. Another one followed in seconds.

"Think they found Finneous," Elijah said.

They reached the top of the bluff. Albert read the road sign: Main Street. He was naked on the busiest street in the city and involved in the newly discovered crime. His heart raced; he could not look up. He wanted to crawl down a hole and disappear, but there were no hides, only people swarming around like ants on an anthill, rushing to their jobs.

"Sit over there on that bench."

Albert pulled his knees up to his chest when he sat down on the bench and wrapped his arms around his legs hoping to disappear. He had sunk to the utter depths. For only a few moments, he had been the hero, and now, a circus freak for people to gawk at for free. Elijah stood on the end of the bench and cleared his throat.

"Our Lord Jesus say: 'Whatever you done to the least of these, you done unto me!'"

Despite the swollen lip and puffed eye, he stood tall and smiled. With his clothes caked in dirt, he appeared as some weird little prophet, and his golden voice carried all over the block.

A man in a brown suit stopped in mid stride and stared. Others slowed and perked their ears. Elijah broke right into stories of people who had risked their lives, losing everything, to save others. There was Hester Grimes who gave her last sack of beans away to a homeless child, and Buck, a hunter who stepped in front of a bear to distract it while an injured friend dragged himself to safety.

Albert doubted if any of the stories were true, but they sounded good, and Elijah's speech was hypnotic. Confidence always exuded from him, but now he brimmed with command. A small crowd gathered, nodding their heads. Some gasped and others spurted "Amen." A tall man in a tie elbowed a pudgy man with glasses and mumbled something about the boy "bringin' it."

"And just last night, I was catfishing–runnin' a trotline in a little chute–catchin' fish like the Lord Jesus commanded us to catch men..."

"Hallelujah!"

"Come on, boy, preach it!"

"And I noticed my line a bouncin'. I had hooked one, a blue. I pulled the line, and I'd swear to you if I'd not known better, I saw Jonah peering out his jaws!" Elijah's eyes beamed wide, and he gestured like he was looking out of a mouth.

Some on-lookers giggled, and a man set down his briefcase and clapped and clasped his hands together as in prayer. A smile ran across his face.

"That Go-liath fish was enough to feed me a month! He writhed and twisted, and not even David could have killed this giant. I reached over my canoe, thanked the Lord for this gift, and pulled, and..."

The crowd went silent, waiting on his word.

"I fell straight in and twisted wit that cat!"

"Oh, Lord, no!" a lady wailed on a park bench. The crowd swooned.

"The line crawled up my arms and 'round my neck and pulled me into the black muddy water."

The sermon was Albert's story –sort of.

"That cat rolled on me, workin' wit all his might, revenging himself for gettin' hooked in his mouth. I went under. I fought to poke my head up for jus' a morsel of air, and I called out to the Lord Jesus, 'SAVE ME!'"

A few men looked at their watches. The women waved fans in front of their faces. Elijah had to hurry.

"Then someone reached down in the depths and lifted me to the top."

He looked at Albert and pointed. "This angel of mercy dove in so hard and fast he done lost his britches in the current." People giggled. "This young man loosened my bonds and lifted me up..."

Then they clapped. Others shouted, "Praise Jeeeesus!"

"This young man, a boy of lighter shade, saved me, a poor black boy! The least of them!"

A soldier nodded and clapped and patted Albert's shoulder.

"Now he's the least of these, and he is a needin' your help. It's jus' like the Lord say: he was naked and you clothed him. Will you help the least of these out? He's lost all he had to save this one lost sheep. Will you minister to the Lord Jesus himself, today?"

A man dug in his pocket and dropped some change in Elijah's cupped hands. Another man reached in his jacket and unfolded a dollar. A large woman, named Eloise, opened her tiny coin purse with her sausage-round fingers and handed Albert a silver dollar. Then a man pushed his way through the people, holding up a pair of overalls. He had gone across the street to the general store and bought a pair. "Hopefully, son, these will fit."

Albert nodded and said thanks, and soon the crowd dissipated, leaving only a few stragglers, and one in particular caught his eye: a policeman. He had been sitting on a bench at the rear of the throng. He smiled and rolled his billy club around in his hand over and over again. Albert breathed fast, his heart felt like it could explode from his chest. They were too suspicious; their plan teetered on failure.

He slipped on the overalls, only able to envision Finneous and that knife in his back.

The officer stood and approached. He was short and stocky, and his nose covered half of his face. He twisted and turned his billy club. Sweat beaded on his forehead under his hat.

"Good sermon. Where you boys from?"

"Frayser," Albert blurted, regretting his quick response. "The Shanties."

"That's quite a ways. You have parents? They know where you're at?"

Albert said nothing. Elijah looked down.

"What's your names?"

"I is Elijah Amos Fortune Jones. This here's Albert McClune."

"Been down by the river?"

They could not lie. Elijah had already talked about his rescue. It may be a trick to see if Elijah had a different story. This was it. Soon they would be cuffed and booked.

"That's where he saved me. Didn't you listen to me and my word from the Good Lord, officer?"

He laughed and said, "Apparently not enough. The wife says I got the same problem at church."

He seemed nice, but Albert hoped he would just go away soon.

"Well, I need to take you boys to the station. Notify your parents that you're safe."

The money would be lost. If they left, someone would eventually uncover it, and it would probably be linked to dead Finneous. It would be celebrated as recovered from Kelly's ransom. They had to get away, but if they ran like before, they would be in trouble. Being barefoot and tired from their adventure meant they would surely be caught. Elijah backed up.

"We ain't got phones, and we's headin' that way. Jus' gonna walk down Second, here."

"That has to be five or six miles, and your feet?" He pointed at them. "You boys ain't got shoes. The station is just down here on Beale."

Turning the corner, a squad car pulled up. The grim officer driving was so tall that his head appeared to scrape the car's ceiling.

"See, here's a ride right here."

The driver leaned out of the window and whispered, "Harris, hop in. A body's been found by the river."

The boys were already gone before the officer could turn. They topped the bluff and headed down the steep sidewalk. People mumbled about the body found and a murderer on the loose. A lady spotted them and waved, "Good sermon young man!" She leaned toward a man and pointed saying something about Albert's rescue of Elijah.

"Too bad they ain't more boys like that one," he responded.

It was ingenious. While the city recoiled at the mysterious murder, Elijah and Albert would no longer be suspicious. They would only be the boys who had been cat-fishing a little far from home. They were heroes, not suspects.

Elijah found the cache, and while Albert kept watch, he shifted the stones and drew out the burlap bag. He checked the cash, and it feathered inside like the guts of a goose down pillow, and Albert could not wait to get his half back home and safe.

As the boys pushed north, heading for home along the river, the city buzzed with news and rumors of the stabbing victim. Elijah and Albert carried the riches of one of the most notorious criminals in the south, and their only enemy was dead and unidentifiable, shrouded in a mystery that would never be unraveled.

Chapter Fifteen

The sun bounced off the muddy water sending sparkling light in every direction. The air was heavy and thick, smelling of sewage and rotten flesh, and every breath was a chore in the pounding heat.

Elijah and Albert trudged along the bank among the river rocks, resting occasionally in the shade of a tree. The brown water swirled, causing a large buoy to bob and lean, shoved down by the river. Albert smiled as a log glided by and spun in the vortex of a small whirlpool.

The river was peaceful, but it was time to push homeward and surprise his family. There would be trouble at first, but it would not matter once they saw the cash.

Memphis drifted behind them as they pushed up river. The landscape changed from open riverbanks and the city perched on the bluff to a thick forest with cliff-like levees and swampy bottoms. Tall reeds lined the bank, and dragonflies zinged in and out, strafing the moving water.

They were only an hour or so from home. It was nice to have the shade of the trees, but it was a challenge to weave in and out and over the eroding bank. Albert slipped on the loose dirt, sliding down into some mud.

Elijah stumbled ahead. It was his turn to carry the money. They had been through so much, and Albert could not think of a better friend.

"Wolf River is up here a piece," Elijah said.

"When you wanna divide the money?"

"I say we's head up the Wolf and find a quiet spot. Hopefully, they ain't no fishin' hap'nin. I think this heat will run them fishes deep away from the hooks."

The tall trees were behind them now, and the mouth of the Wolf River was revealed. Albert had spent countless hours there with Pete running trotlines, tracking raccoon, and playing war along its banks. He snickered to himself at how he had imagined being a Chickasaw warrior, knife in hand, sneaking along the water. It was the best memory he had of Pete. Tears welled up and Albert pushed them back down and wiped his face with his sweat-covered arm. He missed his brother. It would be good to take some of the money, buy a bus ticket, and go for a visit.

"I know a good spot, Elijah, right up by a swinging tree. Pete and I used to swing out into the Wolf when the fishing was bad. If anybody comes down the river, there is a thicket large enough to hide us."

Elijah headed in the direction Albert pointed, looking for the tree.

"Hey Albert? How much of the total treasure you think you took? Half?" Elijah asked, trotting to an old maple tree and yanking on one of the long swinging vines. He glanced back at Albert for approval.

Albert nodded. The vines were long and thick and dangled from high on the bough. The tree hung out over the water, making the area a perfect hideout for boys.

"I don't think I scratched the surface of the treasure; jars were everywhere, but I knew you weren't gonna hold out much longer, so I got all I could."

Albert grabbed the roots sticking out of an eroding bluff behind them and used them like a rope, climbing up the side to the grassy top.

Elijah tossed the bag to him and followed. They relaxed on overgrown, soft rye. Before them were the hanging vines and the slow river, and behind stretched kudzu covered woods. Elijah looked around and reached in the bag.

"Well, you is probably right. I was 'bout ready to call it quits."

The handfuls of money fluttered out like a busted bag of leaves. The bills were crinkly and muddy, but they were all in one piece. Hundreds, maybe thousands of dollars, lay before them.

"We agreed to fifty-fifty. Guess we better get to countin'."

Albert grinned and said, "What did you say you were going to do with your half?"

"Gonna buy my daddy some books of his own and me some too and a pair of shoes. We's gonna eat like kings and be livin' in high cotton!" He slapped his hands and rubbed them together quickly.

"I think I'm gonna buy my momma a new dress and my daddy a suit. He's always sayin' if he had a suit, he'd get a better job, some food of course, and then..."

"Go on, don't stop."

"And I'm going to buy a bus ticket and see Pete at the hospital."

A long silence settled between them, then Elijah nodded and said, "That's a good one, Albert. That's one of the best I've heard."

A crack echoed in the hollow behind them. The boys shuffled the cash back into the burlap and crouched low.

Leaves rustled, kudzu vines popped, tangling on someone's foot. Albert's heart raced again.

"I gotta bead on you. Both of you, hands up! Stand up slowly!"

Time froze. Albert could not move except to look down. He rose slowly like a defeated warrior.

"I SAID HANDS UP!"

Albert heeded. Elijah lifted the bag in one hand and raised the other hand empty.

A big boy and his short stocky partner poked out through a thicket down the hill behind them. They stood in the shadows of the trees, obscuring their faces, but the rifle revealed the big one's identity. Buddy Clines stood just yards away, holding them captive with the gun he had stolen.

"Well, lookie here, JJ. Looks like McClune done got him a nigger."

Albert grit his teeth and clinched his fists.

"Oh, that got him roused, J.J., McClune's turned nigger-lover, may just want to scrap a little. He's a big boy, no doubt, but he's yella."

J.J. snickered and stepped closer with Buddy. Buddy lowered the rifle. "Didn't get enough of me last time? Oh, by the way, thanks for the rifle. Best present I ever got."

They stepped within feet of Albert and Elijah whose arms shook from being raised above their heads. Albert squinted in the glare of the sun, sweat glistening on his forehead and upper lip.

Buddy laughed, "How's your crazy brother?"

Albert snapped and charged and doubled in pain when J.J. met him with an upper-cut to the stomach. Air shot from his mouth and he felt his guts would follow. It was like being under the water again with no air. Everything went dark, and he fell to his knees, gulping for breath.

Buddy gave J.J. the gun and stomped toward Elijah, yanking his arm.

"Whatcha gonna do, Clines, you devil?" Elijah mouthed and spit in Buddy's face. It was the last of his defiance.

Buddy struck him square on the nose, and Elijah wilted, toppling backward off the ledge. Landing on his back, he rolled to the water's edge. Buddy pounced on top of him. Albert came to and squirmed to the ledge to see what would happen.

Buddy dragged Elijah by the hair into the river. "I'm gonna drown me a coon."

Elijah still clutched the burlap which flayed behind him while he was tossed like a rag doll. He was powerless against Buddy. After hitting the water, he wobbled to his feet, blood pouring from his nose.

Albert rose to his knees and heard a click.

"Don't move!"

The bore of his rifle waved before his nose. He swallowed hard. Behind him, water splashed, and shouts of "Swim nigger!" rang through the air, and then there was the silence of Elijah being held under the water.

Albert saw the burlap in the corner of his eye, floating, heading toward the Mississippi while he kneeled, helpless. All at once the faces of Pete, Digger, and Finneous flashed in his mind. He wanted to run. He remembered all the times he had given in to fear, how it hurt others, how he hated himself for it. He mumbled at the memories.

"Risked his life for the least..."

"What? What'd you say, McClune?"

Buddy lifted Elijah's head and screamed in his face and dunked him back under.

"You wouldn't understand. You will never understand," Albert said.

"Understand what?

Albert turned to face J.J. He smiled at the toadie and said, "Why I'm not scared anymore," and he snatched the barrel as a shot echoed through the woods.

Buddy stopped the baptism and turned. There was a long silence. Elijah rolled over in the water, wheezing and hacking.

"You get him J.J.?"

The forest was silent. He waded closer to the bank and peered through the trees.

There was a creak and a flash of denim and a body swinging through the opening. Albert released the vine and flew, crashing on top of Buddy. There was splashing, yelling, swinging, and punching. Buddy was overrun by fury and soon floated face down in the water.

Albert waded over, clinched Buddy's shirt with his left hand, and lifting him up, he pounded with his right fist over and over again. Then he yanked the bully out into the deeper water and shoved his head under like Buddy had been doing to Elijah, like Finneous had done to him.

Drown him. It would do everyone a favor. He lifted him up and plunged him down again.

"Albert, stop!"

He forced Buddy's head under harder. It felt good, powerful. Albert dominated for the first time in his life. He was strong. He was big–a giant. Buddy stopped thrashing.

"Prince Albert, you are a hero! Stop!"

Albert turned, rage twisting his face. He lifted Buddy up. Elijah stood knee deep, stumbling and raising his hand and yelling, "Don't do it. He ain't worth it."

"The hell he ain't!"

"Your soul: it's healed. You're a hero now. You're whole... a new person. Don't tear your soul again."

Albert looked at Buddy. His green eyes rolled around as his head bobbed. He had lost a tooth and blood ran from the black crevice. His face swelled instantly. Elijah waded over and touched Albert's raised fist. Albert hesitated and then lowered it. He unclenched his teeth and dragged Buddy to the bank, tossing him down.

"Oh God! The bag? The money?"

It was gone. Albert sprinted down to the river mouth but saw nothing, and there were no signs of it anywhere. In that bag was all the hope for his family, all of he and Elijah's dreams. He hit his knees—all that work and nothing to show for it. Water ran around his mud stained legs as he trembled.

Elijah limped over to the vine swing and climbed up the bank. Albert pushed himself up and walked back along the bank, and Elijah slid down from the bluff holding the rifle.

"This that famous rifle?"

"It was my grandfather's, from the Great War."

Albert wiped his eyes with his arms and looked at the gun. At least he had it back.

Elijah's face turned serious when he asked, "What happened to J.J.?"

"He ran off. He acted tough, but once the gun fired, it scared him. We'll probably never have trouble from either of them again."

Buddy moaned a little and rolled on his back. The silt from the riverbank clotted in his shaved hair, and the current moved around his legs and feet.

Albert stood over him in silence; he did not have to say anything. He had delivered his message loud and clear that day.

Albert took one last look at the river, wishing with all his might that the burlap would appear, caught up in a fallen tree branch or spattered against a pile of river rock, but it was no use. He turned and clambered up the bank. Elijah followed behind, and the two weaved through the tall oaks and kudzu-blanketed sweet gums sharing nothing but silence.

The rifle had some fresh scars from Buddy's careless use that Albert's dad would not be happy about, but at least it was back in the family. Albert knew that his disappearance would outweigh a few scratches on the stock.

After crossing the train tracks, they reached a potholed gravel road that wound toward a clump of houses. Albert took a deep breath and said, "Well, this is it."

"Which one of them is yours?"

"The last one on the right, the one with the peeling paint. There's an old shed in the back."

"That where you got the pickles?"

"Yep."

"I think you be needin to kill some squirrels before you poison yourself with them things, or use them to poison the squirrels."

Albert chuckled and said, "If they'd eat them."

"Or, we could jus' go a fishin'."

"I'll tie the snoods. I think I do a better job," Albert replied.

The two boys, black and white, shook hands and parted like old friends–Albert to his dilapidated shotgun house and Elijah to the rickety shack in the Shanties.

Chapter Sixteen

The Wolf River was warm after a long hot summer. A gust of wind rustled the tree leaves warning that autumn was on its way. The pointy oaks and maples would soon lose their green and fall, covering the ground with brown, orange, red, and yellow.

There were only a few good weeks of fishing left, then it would be too cold. Albert waded in, something he had not done on his own since Digger's drowning. He pulled up a line and a fish–a channel cat, grey, weighing about five pounds. Wriggling and biting the hook, Albert examined how its belly swelled from foraging. He grabbed the bottom lip, pulled the hook loose, and threw the fish onto the bank, continuing down the line. His backside was still sore from the lashing he had gotten from Dad. He reached back and rubbed it, smiling and snickering at the adventures that perpetrated it.

After clearing the line, he hooked the fish on a stringer and meandered along the bank. He could not help but look. It had become a habit to hope for the impossible. The bag could have sunk and then washed up across a log. It may be around the bend, money all pressed into the mud, ready to be picked out.

Life would be so different with it. The pantry would be full, Dad sporting a new suit, working a new job. Hopefully, less trips to the bar–peace and happiness.

But, there was no money. It had probably sucked to the bottom with the current, or it was floating half way to New Orleans.

Nevertheless, life was different, at least for Albert. He walked the woods and fished the river in peace. He was the "one who kicked Buddy Clines' ass," so when he encountered other boys on the road or river, they either kept their distance or offered a sheepish hello.

He missed Elijah. He only had a few friends but none like him. A week had passed since their adventure, and it was if the little preacher had disappeared, just left the earth. Albert considered waltzing into the Shanties and asking for him, but he had never been there, and he was not sure he would be accepted.

Their adventure was an unforgettable three days. Albert's parents had notified the Sheriff, convinced he had drowned in the river, and so when he showed back up on the front porch, all wet and muddy, he got the lickin' of his life. It was a couple of days before he could look Momma in the eye, and there was no chance of ever telling her he had been treasure hunting (that would probably just bring another whipping).

He decided to stick with the story that he had been running away–that had been his original intention anyway. So he made up a story of hopping a barge and getting kicked off up river as it steamed to Missouri. It was believable. Dad had encountered stowaways countless times, so it seemed plausible compared to the truth.

Zephaniah paddled along the river one afternoon, probably doing his own fishing. Albert started to shout a greeting, to thank him again, but Zephaniah was not one of those people who wanted or expected it. He was a man more happy to be left alone. He nodded and winked, and Albert smiled in return.

After a long day of running trotlines, Albert was starving, so the smell of dinner cooking was a nice welcome when he reached the yard. It was the starchiness of boiling potatoes, maybe even potato soup. He approached the kitchen window, Mom puttered around between some sewing and dinner, her threadbare dress swished, and she moved from pot to sink. Albert cleared his throat and dropped his fish stringer right into the empty sink.

"You expect me to clean them?"

"I caught," he smiled, "you clean?"

She smirked and lifted up the stringer. "I guess. Go into the storeroom and get me some pickles. They'll go good with fried catfish and potatoes."

Albert grimaced at the thought of pickles being a side dish to fish, but he could not complain. He walked around back, his feet crunching in the gravel, and he reached the shed door. Dad was gone up river on a barge and would not be back for days, so he would only need to get one jar.

He stepped around the old carburetors and fan motor and yanked the storeroom door. Reaching in was always a trick because he did not know if he would catch the light string or a spider's web, but thankfully, he found the string and pulled. The dusty light bulb buzzed, then flickered. The pickle jars were scattered along the shelf, but sitting right in between two of them was a single mason jar, splattered with mud. He had never seen the jar in there and wondered if Dad may have misplaced it after one of his drinking fits.

Albert grabbed the jar and spun the band off easily. Then he pried the sealed lid loose. Crammed inside was a twisted slip of paper and wads of muddy money. He pulled out the slip, then the cash—at least a couple of hundred dollars. He unfolded the paper and read:

Albert,
Why is you gettin pickles?!

Been searching the riverbanks for
money. I split what I found fifty-fifty
like we agreed. I got way more than I
bargained for in a biness partner. I got
a friend. Let's go fishin sometime,
without the adventures, please!
Elijah
P.S. Leave the pickles!

Albert giggled and thumbed through the bills
over and over. They were muddy and dry, stiff as if
frozen. He looked around, hoping nobody was
watching him. He had become accustomed to bad
things happening when good things arrived. He was
so excited, he did not know what to do. He read the
note again and thought for a minute, then he grabbed
a jar of pickles and sprinted to the kitchen.

The screen door creaked and slammed behind
him. Momma, sweat beading on her brow, gutted the
fish and threw the entrails out of the window.

"Is Dad gonna be home tomorrow?"

"Probably not, he's on a barge. Be home in
about three days," she said, throwing some guts out

of the window and dropping the slimy fish back into the sink and washing her hands.

The kitchen was like a furnace from the potatoes which now cooled on the stove. Steam rolled out of the pot and gathered in an upside down nest, disappearing.

"Momma, you need a new dress, and I'm gonna buy you one."

She smirked. Not being able to afford a dress in years, she had given up on the idea of anything more than survival. She took the jar from his hands and twisted the top.

"Oh, really, what would I need a new dress for, gutting your catfish?

"To wear to Bolivar, to see Pete," Albert said, slapping each bill onto the table like a poker dealer. "That is, if there's enough after the bus tickets."

He backed into the doorway and stood victorious, just like he and his brother had done so long ago.

Mom dropped the jar of pickles, and it shattered on the floor. The pungent smell of vinegar filled the small kitchen. Her eyes filled with tears, and

then, after years of piled on sorrow, a smile appeared
on her moistened face, because smiling came
naturally in the presence of a hero.

THE END

About the Author

Scott T. Gill
Rockwall, Texas

After serving as a minister for nearly 15 years, Scott Thomas Gill left the "cloth" to pursue a different calling: teaching and telling stories. Now, as a middle school teacher and coach, he helps teens read, instructs writing, and inspires athletes from the sidelines. Outside education, Scott is an avid writer, having been published in *The EFCA Today*, *Dallas Child*, *Teachers of Vision* and compilations such as *Chicken Soup for the Father and Son's Soul*, *Democrat's Soul* and *The Ultimate Teacher*. He lives in Rockwall, Texas with his wife, Angie and their four children.